THE DARK CORNERS

A schoolboy disappears — but the missing child may not be all he seemed . . . A mortician and his family find their new neighbours disturbingly interested in their affairs . . . Quiet Mr. Wooller finds himself the only man ready to take down the Devil . . . An escaped convict stumbles upon an apparently idyllic holiday cottage . . . A spouses' golf game ends in murder . . . In an outwardly perfect marriage, one partner is making dark dealings . . . A young man is subjected to a bizarre hostage-taking . . . Seven unsettling stories from the pen of Robert J. Tilley.

ROBERT J. TILLEY

THE DARK CORNERS

& OTHER STORIES

Complete and Unabridged

LINFORD
Leicester

First published in Great Britain

First Linford Edition
published 2015

A catalogue record for this book is available
from the British Library.

ISBN 978–1–4448–2664–7

Published by
F. A. Thorpe (Publishing)
Anstey, Leicestershire

Set by Words & Graphics Ltd.
Anstey, Leicestershire
Printed and bound in Great Britain by
T. J. International Ltd., Padstow, Cornwall

This book is printed on acid-free paper

Contents

The Dark Corners

A tall hedge concealed the house from the road and the open fields on either side. Beyond it, an unkempt lawn straggled beside the curving driveway that bulged into a half-circle of gravel where it ran across the front of the building. The grey stone of the house itself had almost disappeared, now only visible in shadowed patches among the tangle of ivy that covered it.

'Ideal sort of premises,' Chapman said. He eased into neutral, and let the car coast to a gently crunching halt by the front porch. His bright bird's eyes flicked appraisingly across the clutter of leaves and coarse vines. 'Just about as isolated as anything around here, I should think. Looks as if he might have had something of the sort in mind when he moved in.'

'Except for the fact,' Hull said, 'that he was left it by his uncle. That makes that line of reasoning a bit too complicated for my taste.' He pushed his door open, and swung his feet out onto the gravel. Chapman switched off the ignition, frowning slightly, then followed suit.

Hull mounted the steps leading to the front door, and thumbed the tarnished bell-push that showed among the encroaching greenery. Somewhere inside the house a bell rang faintly, followed immediately by a deep-throated bark.

Chapman paused on the steps, cocking his head. 'Didn't know he had a dog. Sounds like a big one.'

'Yes,' Hull said. He stood with his back to the house, slowly swivelling his head to study the grounds. They were in poor repair. Tufts of grass littered the driveway and the open area of gravel, and the lawn was almost knee-high and flecked with the bright yellow of dandelions. A greenhouse beyond the low privet hedge to their right was starting to weather badly, and the hedge itself was untrimmed.

Inside the house, footsteps clicked towards them. There was a pause, the grating snap of a catch, and the door opened.

The man who peered out at them was

middle-aged and rather stocky, with red hair receding slowly from a freckled forehead. He wore a dark green cardigan over an open-necked shirt, and held a dirty metal dish in his hand. His round, ageless face was very tired.

'Yes?'

Hull said, 'Mr. James Pardoe?'

'That's right.'

'My name is Inspector Hull, and this is Detective-Sergeant Chapman. We would like a few words with you if we may, sir.'

'Oh?' the red-haired man said. His face had tightened, almost perceptibly. 'What about?'

Hull said, 'If we could come inside for just a moment — ' He let his voice trail off, his eyes on Pardoe's face.

'Is that strictly necessary?'

Hull nodded. 'I rather think that it may be.'

There was a pause. Pardoe stared past them, his mouth small and his face thoughtful. Then he shrugged, shook his head slightly, and pulled the door towards him. 'Come in.'

Hull stepped past him into the

shadowed coolness of a tiled corridor, Chapman following. A little way down the passage, a large Alsatian stood, its tongue projecting from the side of its mouth and its eyes fixed brightly on them.

Pardoe closed the door, and said, 'Here, Dan.' The dog jerked into movement, lowering its head and padding to them with relaxed, graceful steps. Pardoe fondled its muzzle, and gestured towards an open door on their left. 'We'd better go in there.'

It was a living room, shabby, and stale with the mingled smells of the dog and cooked food. A cloth covered a small mahogany table, and a used plate sat on it, dull with grease. There was a beaker beside it, and a sauce bottle. Books littered the room, piled precariously on the mantelpiece and the end of a decrepit chaise longue. Yellowed hunting prints were spaced precisely on two of the distempered walls.

'Sit down,' Pardoe said. He put the metal dish on the table, nodding vaguely towards the crockery. 'You'll have to excuse the dishes. I've been rather busy.'

'Quite all right,' Hull said. He seated himself in a worn leather armchair, placing his hat on the carpet beside him. Chapman moved a pile of magazines to the sideboard, and sat on a straight-backed dining chair. Pardoe stood by the table, one hand resting lightly on the dog's head, a look of stiffly polite enquiry on his face.

Hull said, 'Mr. Pardoe, I have to ask you some questions. It shouldn't take very long, but before we start I feel there's something you should be told. Certain information has been brought to our attention that has led us to some pretty damaging conclusions.'

'Really?' Pardoe said. 'Involving me in some way?' His voice, like his face, was courteously empty.

Hull said, 'It appears so, yes. I understand that you are employed as head of the history department at Corley Grammar School.'

'Yes.'

'One of your pupils was a boy called Philip Carver. I say *was*, because of his disappearance two months ago. At that

7

time a colleague of mine questioned you, together with the rest of the staff at Corley. You stated then that you knew nothing at all that might help us with our investigations as to the boy's where-abouts. We drew a blank all round, and until this morning we had no idea at all where he might have got to. Now we're pretty sure we know.'

Pardoe said nothing, but his hand, which had been moving gently on the dog's head, was now quite still. Chapman moved slightly in his chair.

Hull said, 'About a mile from here, there's a farm owned by some people called Hucker. A week ago, the Hucker children, two boys and a girl, say they were in your grounds. They were pretty quiet about it, because they were trespassing, and they took care to keep well under cover. While they were here, they heard a noise, someone shouting. They thought it might possibly be aimed at them at first, so they hid in some rhododendron bushes by the side of the house, and then they say they saw something very odd.' Hull paused, and

8

tilted his head, queryingly. 'Would you like to hazard a guess at what it was, Mr. Pardoe?'

The red-haired man's face was suddenly very pale, and his eyes were closed. He opened his mouth, made a faint sound and then closed it again. He shook his head, very slowly.

Hull said, 'They saw a boy run from this house, followed by a man. The boy looked very frightened, they say, and he was yelling something that could have been a cry for help. He fell in the driveway, and the man caught him. When he'd caught him, he hit him so hard that he almost knocked him unconscious, then he dragged him back inside the house. From their description, it would rather appear that the man was you. Was the boy Philip Carver?'

Pardoe's teeth showed briefly, then his eyes opened. His voice sounded clogged. 'Why did you take so long to get here?'

'The children were frightened, and they didn't tell their parents about it for a couple of days. They'd been trespassing, and children can be a bit funny about things like that. They don't know how to compare values too well at times. When they finally did speak up, their father thought about it for another couple of days before telling us. Grown-ups can be pretty silly, too, but children do make up some weird and wonderful stories.' Hull paused, and cocked his head again. 'Where is he?'

Pardoe said, 'Upstairs.' His voice was almost inaudible and his face was sick. Hull jerked his head at Chapman.

Chapman stood up, and said, 'Is there a key?'

'Wait,' Pardoe said. He took a very deep breath, and leaned back against the table, lowering his hands to its edge. Hull saw them shaking as he gripped it. 'Before you fetch him, I must tell you something.'

'There'll be plenty of time to make a statement when we get to the station,' Hull said. He reached down for his hat. 'I think that the most important thing now is to get — '

'No,' Pardoe said. It was a dryly staccato sound, more an order than a protest. Beside him, the dog growled and stiffened. 'No, you must hear this before we go.'

There was a brief silence in the room. Hull said, 'We have to be sure that the boy is all right first.'

Pardoe frowned, and looked at him, searchingly. 'Then you'll hear what I have to say?'

Hull nodded. 'If you think it's that important. Can you make it short?'

Pardoe shook his head, a rapid, nervous jerking that continued as he talked. 'No, not very. But I must tell it before we get away from here, into a — ' He lifted a hand, and helplessly dropped it again ' — an official atmosphere. This is the only place where it will make sense. At least — ' He stopped, and stared confusedly at the floor.

'You appreciate, of course, that anything you say may be later used in evidence,' Hull said. He looked at Chapman. 'Go and find him, then take him to the kitchen, wherever that is. Make him a sandwich or something, until we're ready.' To Pardoe, he said, 'Is that all right with you?'

Pardoe nodded, silently, then reached into a trouser pocket and produced a Yale key. He handed it to Chapman without looking at him. Chapman took it, and walked to the door. The dog watched him go, poised uncertainly, and then slowly relaxed as he passed out of sight. His feet sounded, mounting the stairs.

There was silence, broken only by the almost inaudible scolding of a bird, somewhere outside the house. Pardoe leaned against the table, his head lowered and his eyes closed. When he started to speak, it was in a flat monotone, a dead voice, that sounded expressionlessly in the thick-atmosphere confines of the room.

'My reason for coming to this part of the country was this house. My uncle died just over eighteen months ago and left it to me, and I came down from Bradford, where I was teaching, simply to look it over before selling it. I liked it, despite the fact that it was really much too big for a single man, and I decided I'd like to keep it. I had a vague idea at the time that I might be able to turn it into two flats, or something of the kind, but I decided later that I preferred the idea of solitude. The job at Corley was advertised two months afterwards, and I got it and moved in here at the beginning of the winter term. That was ten months ago, and the first time that I met Philip Carver.'

Hull interrupted, 'Perhaps you'd better sit down. You look rather shaky.'

'Yes,' Pardoe said. He walked to the chaise longue, pushed some books to one side, and sat down, resting his arms horizontally across his thighs. The dog crossed the room to him, sniffing impersonally at the carpet, then slumped loosely at his feet, its eyes closed. Pardoe continued speaking in the same dull, disinterested tone.

'He was in the upper fourth form when I first knew him. His reputation was a not-unusual one among boys of that age. He produced spurts of brilliance in his work, but he was erratic. His most notable feature was a genuine oddity, though, but not recognised as such by many members of the staff. The majority seemed satisfied to refer to him as a toady, but they were rather missing the point. He seemed to have the knack of anticipating people's wants to a remarkably accurate degree. I noticed this myself soon after I started, and it puzzled me, certainly more so than the rest of the people there. As I say, they were inclined to dismiss him as a fairly standard sort of boot-licker, but I became rapidly convinced that he was something much more than that.'

He paused. Above them, there was the slam of a door, and then, very faintly, the sound of voices. He ran his tongue across his lips, and blinked once.

'I finally caught him out during a mock school certificate exam. I hadn't consciously laid a trap, or anything like that, but under the circumstances it was hardly surprising that he blundered. The paper was a very general thing, dealing with no particular period of history, that I'd concocted rather hurriedly on the evening prior to the exam. That's the way these things usually happen: they're supposed to be prepared two or three weeks before, but they always seem to get delayed for one reason or another. There was some sickness among the staff at that time, and it was necessary to take quite a few extra classes. I hadn't time to get it typed and duplicated, so I was going to write the questions on the blackboard. When I got to the room where the class was waiting for the exam, I had two monitors distribute pens, ink, and foolscap paper to each boy. While this was being done, I checked through the questions that I was going to put to them. I was half-way through doing this, checking them against the answers, when the headmaster's secretary appeared. She said that if I hadn't already started the exam, would I please go and see the head immediately. I went, taking the question paper with me.'

The footsteps that had been slowly descending the stairs stopped. Hull heard Chapman's voice, querying, followed by a muttered, hesitant reply.

The dog's head snapped up. Slowly, it uncurled and rose, its eyes fixed rigidly on the open doorway. Pardoe reached out a hand to its head, patting it very slowly and gently. He smiled bleakly at Hull, saying nothing.

Chapman appeared in the doorway. He looked briefly at Hull and Pardoe, then back up the stairs. He said, 'Come on, son, it's all right. There's nothing to be afraid of.' His voice was loud, and very cheerful.

There was a pause, then dragging footsteps sounded again. Hull watched the doorway, conscious of Pardoe's mask-like smile, and his hand, still moving rhythmically on the dog's head.

The boy was thin and very pale, and he looked none too clean. He wore a grey flannel suit that was very crumpled, with a blue-and-yellow badge on the breast pocket of the jacket. He was rather plain, and pimples discoloured his chin and forehead. He stared at Pardoe, saying nothing.

Hull said to him, 'How are you, son?'

The boy moved his gaze from Pardoe, and looked at Hull. He seemed not to have heeded the question, then said, 'Very well, thank you,' rather abruptly. His eyes moved back to Pardoe's bleak, polite smile, and he frowned.

Hull nodded to Chapman. 'Take him along and get him something to eat. We shan't be very long.'

'Right,' Chapman said. He touched the boy's shoulder. 'Let's go and see what there is in the pantry, shall we?'

After a moment, the boy nodded, then turned away without speaking. As he moved out of sight, Hull saw the look of puzzlement on his face, and the final rapid flick of his eyes towards Pardoe. Chapman followed him out of sight, his uncomfortably genial grin still in position.

Hull looked back at Pardoe. The smile was still there, but it held a hint of exhaustion now, and the movement of his hand appeared as more of a dying reflex than a deliberate action.

Hull said, 'What happened when you got there?'

Pardoe shut his eyes, then opened them again. When he spoke, his voice was quiet and very tired, but it contained expression now.

'The head produced the copy of the

exam paper that I'd left with him after assembly that morning, and told me that something seemed to have gone rather amiss. He asked if, before I'd prepared my questions, I'd checked back through the papers set by my predecessor. I confessed that I hadn't, due to circumstances of work. He then pointed out that, in fact, my paper contained several questions that were very similar to some that had been put to the same boys on previous occasions, two of them no more than a year before. He has a quite exceptional memory, and it was just the sort of thing that he would recollect. In view of this oversight, he suggested that the easiest solution to the problem would be to use a paper that had originally been put five years ago, before any of the present pupils had been at the school. I agreed to this, apologised for the trouble that was being caused, and then he had his secretary fetch the old paper from the files. We checked it as quickly as we could, and found that this time none of the questions appeared to be suspect.'

Pardoe continued his gentle massaging

of the dog's head, a faint spark of animation beginning to show in his face as he talked.

'I took the paper back to the classroom, and started to write the new questions on the blackboard. While I was doing this, the piece of chalk that I was using broke. I turned to my desk to get another piece, and saw Carver slipping something into his inside jacket pocket. I told him to bring it out to the front of the class and give it to me.' He hesitated, briefly. 'I've never seen an expression on anyone's face like the one that I saw then. It was a compound of terror and rage, and I was very startled by it. He stayed where he was until I told him again, much more forcefully the second time. Then he came out and handed it to me. It was a piece of foolscap, and written on it were the answers to the first two questions on my original question paper.'

Hull frowned, looking sharply at him.

'Where was the first paper?'

'I left it in the headmaster's study when I brought the alternative paper back with me.'

'And you say you prepared the first paper the night before the exam. Where did you do it?'

'Here.'

'And you're convinced in your own mind that it would have been impossible for this boy or anyone else to have seen it before you took it to the classroom that morning?'

'Utterly impossible.'

Hull said, flatly, 'Then what are you actually saying? That the headmaster left his copy lying around for anybody to pick up, or that the boy is a mind-reader?'

'He can read minds, yes,' Pardoe said.

Hull watched him for a long, silent moment, his face impassive. The dog yawned, a cavernous exercise that concluded with a muffled snap as its jaws closed. It slumped again, its chin resting across its forelegs.

Hull said, 'What happened then?'

'I told him to go back to his seat, then I finished writing the questions on the board. I watched him while the exam was in progress. He wrote nothing, simply sat there staring at me for the better part of two hours. When it was over, I had the papers collected and told him to stay behind when the others had gone. When we were alone, I asked him if it was true.'

'That he was a mind-reader?'

Pardoe nodded. 'Yes.'

'What did he have to say for himself?'

'He admitted it.'

Hull's eyebrows lifted. 'Just like that?' He fumbled his pipe from his pocket, and tucked it into a corner of his mouth. 'Did you believe him?'

'Of course.' Something like anger showed in Pardoe's eyes. 'Don't you see? I *had* to believe him. This was the culmination of it all, the label for the hundred and one demonstrations that I'd witnessed and been so puzzled by. His anticipation of things, his never-failing — *preparedness*. He knew what to do in any situation that involved dealing face to face with an opposite party.' He stared down at the carpet, his hand automatically reaching for the supine figure of the dog.

'I asked him if he really realised what this meant. He said yes. His facial expression when he said it was the most complex thing I've ever seen; contempt, malice, hatred, triumph, they were all there, and others, besides. I asked him to tell me about it, and he did. He told me what it was like for a seeing person to live in a world of the blind, where everything was etched in detail for him and only him. He talked about the unbelievable dirt of the human mental condition, and the fear and ignorance and pathetic fumbling in the darkness of not knowing. He talked about man's lack of faith in man and how it justified itself by its existence, and the stupidity of commitments to unseen gods. Then he went on to tell me how he used these things.'

Hull watched him as he talked, sensing desperation and resignation in the tableau, the quietly talking man and the limp animal at his feet, the stale and shabby book-littered room, thick with the afternoon heat. Just how sane is he? Hull wondered. He searched for his lighter, his eyes steady on Pardoe's dulled, waxy face.

'He used them as a tool, a procuring instrument. When he wanted something, he probed with his mind until he knew the best way to get it. He exploited misfortune, guilt and circumstance as it suited him, using anyone around him that could assist with his requirements of the moment. He described several instances of how he'd done this. The one that particularly stuck in my mind involved his sister. She's a year older than him, and left school last year. Carver knew that she'd been out with various boys, and on one occasion had let rather more happen than was really wise. He wanted money at the time, I forget what for. He told her that he'd seen what happened on the particular evening involved, and unless she got hold of five pounds for him, he would see to it that their father was told. She got it by taking two pounds from her father's wallet, and the rest from other girls' clothing in the gymnasium dressing room. Since then, he's used her as a steady source of income whenever his interests of the moment have required financial investment.'

Hull said, 'Assuming for the sake of argument that all this is true, there's one thing that puzzles me. Harking back to the time of the exam, how was it that he came to write those wrong answers at all, since he must surely have known that you were out getting a substitute set, or, alternatively, why didn't he destroy the paper before you got back with them?'

Pardoe said, 'His range seems to be relatively limited. He wouldn't admit it at first, but I later found out that his effective reading area is somewhere around fifteen to twenty feet. The headmaster's study is on the far side of the building, and I was back in the room before he fully realised what was going on. He was picking up a lot of random interference from the rest of the class, too, of course.'

Hull inclined his head, clicked his lighter, and commenced to puff his pipe alight. 'All right. Then what?'

'When he'd finished telling me all this, I asked him if he simply intended to go on abusing his ability in the same sort of way. He laughed at this. He pointed out that since he had us, the fumbling, blind people, firmly by the throat, and quite unable to take any form of legal action to stop him, to abandon his present thoroughly pragmatic use of his talents would be quite senseless. What would he gain by it? His outburst of confidence, he admitted, had been largely induced by the circumstances in which he'd been trapped. It was a chance for him to boast about his power, and in the confines of the classroom, he felt perfectly safe in telling me what he did. Once outside again, of course, he would simply deny anything that I chose to make public.' Pardoe paused, briefly.

'He also told me that if I made a statement of any kind, he would retaliate with an accusation of attempted indecency and subsequent malicious slander. Despite the fact that he was confident that any awkwardness caused by my production of the written answers could be bluffed aside, he would simply prefer to be spared the trouble. In my own interests, therefore, I would be wise to destroy the only piece of evidence that could support such a claim on my part.'

Hull said, 'He'd have a job proving anything himself, of course.'

Pardoe smiled, thinly. 'That's true, but

he knows more than enough about the workings of human nature. In the case of his own, much more credible story, people's imaginations and ingrained suspicions would accept it as readily as they would dismiss mine.' His face showed no bitterness. 'Anyway, I eventually told him that he could go, and he did. I sat there for a long time, an hour at least. The caretaker was late making his rounds that evening, and it was only his arrival that snapped me out of the daze that I was in. When I left, though, I knew what I had to do. He had to be taken to a place where it would be impossible for him to continue to prey on anyone that he chose. I had a wild hope that if he could be isolated from the dirt and greed and exposed to nothing but pure theory for a time, his mind would still be open enough to accept the sense of a balanced social order and all the curtailments that are essential ingredients of it.'

Hull grunted noncommittally. 'How did you get him out here?'

'He lives some way out of the town, as you know. I followed him to the cinema that evening, and then home again. He was riding a bicycle, and I had my estate car. I kept my distance until we were clear of the houses, then when the road was free of traffic I pulled up to him and ran him into the hedge. Before he had a chance to untangle himself, I was out of the car and had a chloroform pad over his face. Then I put him and the bicycle in the car and brought him here.'

'Very efficient,' Hull said, drily. He squashed the dottle in his pipe with a heavy finger, and flicked his lighter again. 'I take it no traffic passed you while all this was going on.'

'No, none. When I got back here, I took him up to the attic where he's been ever since. I had to keep him tied up for the first couple of days while I soundproofed the room and bricked up the window, because otherwise he might easily have broken his neck trying to climb down a drainpipe, or something of the sort. I took all the furniture out of the room, too, just leaving a camp-stool and a sleeping-bag. I didn't think it wise to leave anything heavier that he might try to knock the door down with.

'When I'd done all this, I untied him and talked to him, and explained why I was doing it, a foolish procedure under the circumstances. He let me finish, and then spat at me and told me he knew all my pathetic reasons and precisely what he thought of them. I asked him if he failed to see the logic behind a disciplined society, and he told me no, he could see it very clearly. But what he could see even more clearly was the flimsiness of the façade that made such things possible, and the incurable weaknesses of the structures themselves. I tried to reason with him for the rest of the week-end, but he simply spat, or screamed or cried. I had to leave him alone, eventually. I left books with him when I went to school on the Monday, hoping that out of sheer boredom he would read them and that some fragment of their reasoning would touch him. When I got back, he'd ripped them to pieces.'

'How did he get out the other day?'

Pardoe's smile was bitter. 'He fooled me. It was bound to happen eventually.

About a fortnight ago, his attitude seemed to be changing slightly, for the better. The hysterics had gone, and he seemed to be listening to what I was saying when I talked to him. One day, he asked for some books. I'd stopped giving him any after the first week; they all ended up in pieces, and there didn't seem to be a lot of point in wasting them — until he showed some indication that they might be read instead of mutilated. I was overjoyed, but cautious, of course. I gave him one or two, and it was obvious from later conversation that he'd actually read at least parts of them. He asked for others, and I gave them to him, which was where I made my mistake.' Pardoe shrugged, almost apologetically.

'One of them was a dictionary; a rather large, heavy item. He dropped some other books that I was handing him at the time, and he made as though to pick them up. Stupidly, I bent down to help him, and he hit me across the neck with it. He didn't knock me out, but I was dazed for a few seconds. He snatched the key from my jacket pocket, unlocked the door, and then he was out. It was his intention to lock me in, but I was on my feet and at the door while he was still trying to get the key into the keyhole. He panicked and ran, and I caught him when he fell outside the house.' He paused. 'You know about that, of course.'

'Yes,' Hull said. He picked with a fingernail at some exposed strands that showed through the arm of his chair. 'So in fact you've made no real progress with him at all.'

'No', Pardoe said. He sounded suddenly and utterly exhausted.

'And what were you planning to do with him if this continued for, say, another two or three months, with no evidence of any headway?'

Pardoe shook his head over his limply interlaced hands. 'I don't know.'

Hull watched him, biting thoughtfully on his pipe. The dog stirred by Pardoe's feet, whined fitfully, then looked around the room with heavy eyes. Watching it, Hull said, 'What do you know about his background?' He lifted his gaze to Pardoe's suddenly blank look. 'Do you

30

know anything at all about his parents, his home life? Has he volunteered anything himself?'

After a pause, Pardoe said, 'It's not too good, from what I've heard at the school. I've tried to sound him out once or twice, but he wouldn't talk about it.'

Hull nodded. 'I'm not altogether surprised to hear it. His mother pushed off with some chap a few years back, and his father's in and out of jobs almost as often as he's in the pub.' He busied himself with the lighter again.

'Assuming still that you're telling me the facts as you see them, it just occurs to me to wonder which way he'd have jumped if he'd had a stable sort of home, some sort of reasonable example set him all this time.' He tucked the lighter away. 'What would you say about it?'

Pardoe's tongue appeared, briefly moistening his lips. 'It may even have been the beginning of it.'

'What?'

Pardoe jerked his head, a nervously impatient dismissal. 'I didn't quite mean that. But I have wondered a lot about cause and effect, the actual reasons for it happening.' He spoke more rapidly now, a faint flicker of brightness showing far back in his eyes. 'Just suppose that in fact the entire human race is on the brink of some evolutionary breakthrough: the gradual opening out of the part of our brain that we've never been able to categorise or map. Perhaps what you've just said is the key. Deprivation has caused him to seek some sort of consoling factor, a kind of refuge that only he can enter. He may have somehow jumped the gun, or discovered a shortcut, if you like, activated entirely by a lack of affection and understanding.' His eyes locked with Hull's, and Hull saw that the brightness was a glint of fear.

'This is only theorising, but suppose I'm right? Do you realise what it means? It means that in all the dark corners of the world, uncountable millions of them, something similar may be happening. Children may be growing up possessed of the same talent, and because of their immaturity, the unformed standards of adolescence, they see it only as a means of acquisition and revenge — ' He jolted to an abrupt halt, his eyes gradually re-focussing on Hull's watchful face. He pushed a faintly vibrating hand across his mouth.

Hull said, 'Then he doesn't claim to have been born like it.'

'No,' Pardoe said, dully. He moved his feet slightly, as though they ached. 'As far as he can remember, it started about three or four years ago. It began very gradually, from what I can gather.' For the first time his voice held a note of tired uncertainty. 'As to what he actually is, I simply don't know. He may be the next stage in our evolutionary programme, or he may be a sport, some kind of throwback. Perhaps he's just a freak.' He lifted his head and stared at Hull, his eyes betraying a muted something that was hard to define.

'But whatever he is, he's dangerous. No more dangerous person ever lived. He's a raging megalomaniac already, and he's incurable. Psychiatry could do nothing for him, because he sees beyond the confines of reason as we know it. He has the world in the palm of his hand, and it's only a matter of time before he learns how to close his fingers around it.'

There was a long silence in the room. Hull stirred, reached over to a nearby table, and carefully tapped his pipe in a bulky ceramic ashtray. He returned it to his pocket, then reached down for his hat. 'That is the lot, I take it?'

Pardoe nodded. His face was rigid, and his eyes were slightly glazed.

'What do you think will happen?'

'To you?' Hull said. He shrugged. 'It isn't my job to speculate on the possible outcome of court action. Whatever the charges eventually are, you can't deny that you've broken the law.'

'The law,' Pardoe said. Sudden disgust and anger choked his voice. 'Don't you realise that what you're doing at this moment is letting loose the worst lawbreaker that ever lived, an incurable abuser of privacy, decency, and all the man-made rules that have enabled societies to be built that contain at least some element of justice?' He was white and shaking. 'Don't you see that?'

Hull fiddled with the brim of his hat.

He said, slowly, 'If what you say about him is true, it's hardly his fault. Someone like that is bound to make their own rules.'

Pardoe stared at him, appalled. 'But don't you see what you're saying? You're admitting that I'm right, but you're still permitting it to happen!'

'You might be right, in theory at least; but even if I knew it to be fact, what could I do about it?' Hull said. He rose, set his hat on his head, and tugged it into position. 'As it is, I don't know whether I believe you or not. Perhaps I do, but whether anyone else will is another matter. Not that it will make a great deal of difference, either way.' He looked vaguely apologetic.

'No,' Pardoe said. He rose slowly to his feet. 'No, of course not.' His voice had changed again, and now Hull heard fear and saw it mirrored in his face, mingled with strangely formal regret. 'It would be too much to expect, of course. Dan, watch him.'

Startled, Hull swung his head towards the dog as it lurched growling to its feet.

There was a blur of movement to his right. Hull stepped back, abruptly, jerking up an arm in a reflex protective action, just in time to block the clumsily wielded sauce bottle that splintered heavily against his elbow. Sudden vertigo threw him off-balance. He pitched on all fours, pawing feebly for Pardoe's legs, sickly aware of the snarling breath of the dog by his face. He heard Pardoe's snapped command, a flurry of movement, then the abrupt slam of the door.

He levered himself to his feet, enormous pressure weighting the back of his head and blurring his vision. He stumbled to the grate, grabbed the poker that lay there, then moved unsteadily towards the corridor. Somewhere near, Chapman shouted furiously, his voice mingling with the thud of a closing door.

At the far end of the passage, the Alsatian had its jaws locked on Chapman's right forearm. Chapman was behind and astride it, his free arm locked around its neck. Beyond them was a closed door. There was no sign of either Pardoe or the boy.

Hull went forward, the poker raised. Chapman stared up at him, then swung his leg free of the dog and backed away, his caught arm stiff and straight. Hull clubbed the dog, heavily. It staggered, whining, and Chapman cried out, buckling against the wall. Hull swung again, and the dog went down. Chapman went with it, his face chalky, and his free hand pulling feebly at its lower jaw.

Hull blundered across the prone body of the Alsatian, and wrenched at the handle of the door. It was locked. He backed, braced himself with a hand on either wall, and kicked heavily beside the lock.

The door crashed open to reveal a stone-floored kitchen. The boy stood at the far end, pressed back against the sink, his face working convulsively and his eyes closed. There was a bread-knife in his hand, half its blade discoloured with blood.

Pardoe was on the floor at his feet. He lay in a foetal curve on his left side, one hand buried against his stomach, the other groping for the boy. As Hull watched, the spread fingers suddenly relaxed and the hand fell.

Hull put the poker on the table, moved across the room, and gently took the knife from the boy's hand.

The boy's eyes were open now, staring blankly down at Pardoe. He offered no resistance as Hull took him by the arm and steered him around the body to a chair in the far corner of the room.

'Don't look at him,' Hull said. He went to the sink, and filled a glass that was upturned on the draining-board. He took it back to the boy and handed it to him, then went back and knelt by the still figure on the floor.

Pardoe was still alive, but his eyes were gradually filming and his pulse was barely detectable. His eyes moved, very slightly, touched on Hull's face, then fell away again. Seconds later, he was dead.

As Hull rose to his feet, Chapman appeared in the doorway, gripping his injured arm. There was blood between his fingers, and his face was wet and sick. He stared at Pardoe's body, then at the boy, his mouth slackly open.

'Oh, Christ,' he said, faintly. He leaned

against the door frame, his head back and his eyes closed.

'We'd better get a tourniquet on that arm,' Hull said. 'Here, let's have your jacket off.' He eased off Chapman's coat, and tied his handkerchief above the elbow of the bleeding arm. 'How's the dog, by the way?'

'Dead,' Chapman said. His eyes went past Hull to Pardoe's huddled body, then he gasped, winced, and closed them again.

Hull seated him in a chair opposite the boy, then went back into the corridor, peering into rooms until he found a telephone. He called the hospital first, then his office.

'You'd better send out a spare driver, too. Chapman can't drive, and I don't really feel up to it.'

He put the phone down, looked briefly out of the window, swore, then went to look for a blanket. He took one from the first bed that he found, carried it down to the kitchen, and spread it across the body. Chapman and the boy were still seated where he had left them, the boy hunched and staring sightlessly at the floor, his hands locked on the tumbler. Chapman watched him with exhausted eyes.

Hull took a second glass from a cupboard, filled it, and proffered it to Chapman. Chapman declined it with a faint shake of the head. Hull leaned against the kitchen table, sipping gently at the water and watching the boy.

After a while, the boy said without looking up, 'He tried to kill — ' His voice thickened, and he stopped.

'It's all right,' Chapman said, brusquely. 'It's all right.' He turned his head towards Hull, his drawn face white and angry. 'You couldn't help it, we know that. Don't we,' he said to Hull.

Hull nodded, shortly, took another sip of water, and looked back at the boy again. His face was quite empty, devoid of expression and movement, faint colour showing again around his rather prominent cheekbones.

God Almighty, Hull thought with sudden irritation. You'd think he'd at least have cried by now.

Perhaps a quarter of a minute passed.

Then, as he watched, a tear showed on the boy's face, leaking jaggedly down one cheek. His face crumpled, and he began to sob.

'Here,' Chapman said. He pushed himself awkwardly forward in his chair, fumbling his good hand into his trouser pocket. He cursed, still searching, and twisted his head towards Hull. 'Give the kid a handkerchief, can't you? Mine must be in my other pocket.' His voice was angry.

Hull put down his glass, took the folded handkerchief from his breast pocket, and walked across to the boy. He held it out to him.

As he took it, the boy looked up, and for a brief moment Hull saw his eyes, watching him from behind the film of water that covered them. Then the tears welled again, and the eyes were gone, masked behind the handkerchief that the boy pressed against them.

'That's right, son, have a good cry,' Chapman said, hoarsely. His voice was at once conciliatory and furious. 'Let it all out, it'll make you feel better.' He sat back in his chair, breathing heavily. After a moment, he turned his attention to Hull, still standing looking fixedly down at the boy's bowed head and shoulders. He shifted irritably in his chair, seeking a point of focus for his restless anger. 'You'd expect him to cry, all things considered, wouldn't you?' he said. His voice was rebelliously querulous. 'It's only natural, isn't it?'

Hull continued to stare, shadows of recent memory flitting greyly through his mind. He thought about Pardoe, a solitary man who believed that he had found a terrifying evil, a belief that had eventually created its own tormented sense of purpose. Was this what he had really found? Were his conviction and speculations grounded in wildly improbable fact, forecasting the inexorable growth of something dark and cancerous that would one day insinuate its malignancy into places of power, or were they the fantasies of loneliness, paranoid dreams that had been woven around the tawdry but easily rationalised trickery of a child?

And if he had been right, Hull

reluctantly went on to question his sense of reasoning, what then? Did others like the boy really exist in the shadowed places of the world, their strange talent somehow prematurely spawned by their emotionally barren circumstances and already warped beyond repair? Were they even then engaged in the petty stratagems of adolescence, the measure of their activities as yet confined by the boundaries of imagination and experience; but slowly, like the opening of some dark and deadly flower, awakening to awareness of the power that they could some day hold?

Dimly aware of Chapman's pugnaciously repeated question, he listened to the keening sobs that came from the boy, his ears straining with unwilling urgency to the texture of their sound, inescapably conscious of the choking pressure of the fear that was clamped coldly and tightly to his throat and stomach.

'Yes,' he said slowly, after a long moment. 'Yes, I suppose it is.'

Fiends and Neighbours

'And,' said my wife, concluding the day's domestic news, 'we have some new neighbours.'

I was, I must admit, a trifle surprised. The previous tenant of the house next door had disappeared some months ago under circumstances that the police had chosen to term 'mysterious'; since which time a trickle of rather obviously dubious clients had spasmodically appeared in the company of an overly-enthusiastic, but in each case unsuccessful, estate agent. We are, it is true, a little isolated and rather far from the main road, but the town is rapidly growing and only four miles away, and a pretty regular country bus service is available.

Personally, I prefer to be cut off from the eternal bustle of people — once the daily grind is completed, it's a good feeling to relax in the company of one's own family secure in the knowledge that

47

we're really too far to be bothered with socially. And in any case, when you're in charge of the local mortuary, as I am, people find plenty of excuses for not wanting to mix with you in your spare time — family memories, and a generally queasy feeling about spending their time with someone who handles cadavers as part of his job, no doubt. Anyway, my wife, since I was fortunate enough to marry the right sort of partner, shares my views on the social side of things, and our son David likes the rural life well enough, so we don't miss what would very probably be a rather irritating series of relationships.

The business of our previous neighbour, a rather odd old chap called Broom, had received a certain amount of publicity in the local press, but not too much fuss had been made about it. There was absolutely no evidence of foul play, and after a couple of weeks it died a natural death. After all, people disappear all the time in very much the same way; and while I think the local police would have liked to carry the matter further than they did, they had very little to work on. Still, you know how it is in a largely rural area. People talk because they have precious little else to occupy their spare time, and some pretty wild conclusions are reached in the process. There was even a short period when my wife and I were subjected to some rather overly obvious close scrutiny from our fellow travellers on our journeys to town; but, thank God, that didn't last very long.

However, as I say, it was rather a surprise. I think the estate agent had more or less written the place off as a white elephant, and we had rather got used to having no immediate neighbours.

'A family?' I asked.

My wife shook her head.

'Two men,' she said. 'One tall, pale and silent, the other short, sandy and also silent. They're both rather grim-looking, and the tall one has very piercing eyes.'

I laughed. My wife has a slight tendency to dramatize about people. I think she'd even rather enjoyed the fuss that had been made about old Broom.

'How do you know they're silent?'

'They came round to borrow some milk.'

'They?' I looked at her, puzzled. 'Did it take two of them to carry a bottle of milk? Provided you gave them one, of course.'

She shrugged.

'Perhaps they're shy. Anyway, the tall one did the talking, what there was of it. He said they hadn't had time to make arrangements with the local tradesmen, but they'd take care of it in the morning. He said they didn't expect to be there for long. Probably only a week or two, depending on circumstances.'

'He still doesn't sound very silent to me,' I said.

'Oh, that was all he said, apart from 'good morning'. The rest of the time he just stood there, giving me the benefit of his piercing glance. I told him how long it was since we'd had anybody next door, and how the estate agents have had such a hard time finding anyone willing to occupy a house with such a mysterious past. He didn't say anything at all — just nodded every so often and fixed me with those penetrating eyes.'

'Well, let's hope they weren't capable of penetrating too far,' I said. 'And what did Lou Costello do all this time?'

She laughed.

'Oh, he just stood there holding the milk bottle. I didn't tell you about his eyes, did I? Rather pale and fishy, and he never blinks. He stared at me, too, but it wasn't half as effective as the other one.' She frowned a little. 'They're an odd couple. I wouldn't say they were exactly creepy, but they both had a sort of — well — slightly fanatical look about them.'

'There are different types of fanatics,' I said. 'They might be musicians or painters or something. Anyway, as long as they don't pester us for milk all the time, they can be as fanatical as they like.'

I yawned and stretched. I hadn't had a particularly hard day — the local mortality rate is pretty low — but there are times when it's an extra-good feeling to be away from the people, live and dead, who surround me all day, and back with those I can really relax with.

I pushed my chair back.

'I think I'll wander round the garden for a bit. I want to have a look at those cauliflowers, and there's always the chance I might get a look at these odd neighbours of ours.' I smiled. 'Shan't be long.'

'All right,' said my wife. She started clearing dishes off the table. 'Don't forget to look at the chickens while you're out there. They've got into the habit of laying an extra egg or two when we're not looking, and then tucking them away in an odd corner where we aren't likely to find them. And I could do with some potatoes for the morning.'

'Chickens and potatoes,' I said, dutifully.

It was fresh in the garden, cool but very pleasant. It was getting dark, so I checked on the chickens while I could see what I was doing. Apparently this was one of their lazy days. They gave a few hostile clucks at being disturbed, but no eggs were forthcoming. I made sure the padlock on the door was firmly locked — you never know what might try creeping in there at night — and fetched the spade from the tool-shed.

It was quite dark when I started digging. I'd sneaked a look over the fence on my way to the potato patch, but nothing was visible in the gloom of the next garden and there were no lights on in the house. I presumed our neighbours were either out or liked to retire early. As a result, it gave me more than just a slight jolt when I suddenly found myself bathed in a pool of white light as I was bent down, feeling for potatoes in the freshly turned ground.

I straightened up and turned slowly, shading my eyes and blinking a little in the glare. The light was directed from the top of the fence that divided the two gardens. It seemed to be coming from a torch or bicycle lamp, and a pretty powerful one at that. I stuck my head forward, squinting at the source, still blinking and wondering who the devil was trying to be funny.

'Yes?' I said. It sounded damned silly at the time, but the whole thing was so unexpected that I couldn't think of anything else to say that wouldn't have involved a certain amount of exasperated blasphemy.

I finally made out a head, silhouetted against the remains of the fading sunset. The torch seemed to be resting on top of the fence, and as far as I could make out he was giving me a thorough once-over.

'Yes?' I said again, and it didn't sound any more intelligent than the first time. I moved forward, still holding the spade, and tried to get a better look at him.

'Digging, I see,' he said, and there was some consolation to the fact that his opening remark sounded as asinine as my own. It was a deep voice, with pretty sombre overtones, and for some reason I was immediately reminded of an under-taker that I'd once known. It had very much the same sort of foreboding note about it.

'Yes,' I said. 'That's right. Digging. For potatoes.' I said it pretty shortly, because the confounded man had nearly made me jump out of my skin. 'I take it you're one of the chaps my wife was telling me about. Our new neigh — '

'Potatoes,' he said, and it sounded like 'bodies'. I don't know if he thought that grave-digging was included among my duties. 'Do you often dig for potatoes at this time of night, Mr. — ah — Brown?'

'When they're needed,' I said. Now that the initial shock had abated a little, I was beginning to feel more than a little resentful. Also, I have always considered the name Brown to be a perfectly presentable one, and his exaggerated pause in the middle of producing it had smacked more than a little of disdain.

'While I appreciate this early attempt at a neighbourly introduction, Mr. — ah — ' He let that one slide. ' — I must confess to a slight allergy to being spotlighted in such an abrupt manner.' I smiled, and made it pretty sour. 'You'll have to excuse what might seem to you my unreason-ableness in this matter, but it's just that I'm not used to . . . '

'Not at all,' he said. 'Your allergy. I quite understand.' He seemed to be playing his torch a little closer to my feet than my face, and his head was tipped a little as though studying the ground. I looked down. A potato gleamed whitely where the spade had neatly sliced it in half. I bent down, picked it up, and waved it gently in the beam of the torch.

'Potatoes,' I said.

He said nothing, and I could feel his eyes probing at me from behind the beam. Then, as abruptly as it had been switched on, the light went out. There was the faintest rustle of grass behind the fence, and then he was gone.

I stood for several seconds, just staring foolishly at the spot above the fence that he had vacated. It was very quiet, and I heard his feet as he reached the gravel path. Then another pair joined in. Together, they crunched off into silence. A door slammed.

Suddenly, the night seemed a lot colder.

Annoyed, puzzled, and with the faintest flicker of fear worming its way down my spine, I finished digging up the potatoes. It was pretty dark, particularly after peering for so long into the beam of light, and I must have split quite a few more before I finally got as many as we'd need for the next day. I took the spade back to the shed, and carried them indoors, frowning.

My wife was reading in the one easy chair that we keep in the kitchen, and she looked up as I came in.

'You've been a long time,' she said. She saw my frown, raised her eyebrows, and put down her book. 'Something wrong?'

I told her what had happened, including the bit about the second pair of footsteps. Before I had finished, she was frowning, too.

'Did you get a look at him?'

'With him shining that confounded light at me, I couldn't see a thing. I must admit, though, more than once I got the impression that you must be right about his piercing eyes. I felt the damned things digging into me at unpleasantly regular intervals. Or maybe it was the little one, peeping through a convenient knot-hole.' I took my pipe from the mantel, and started packing it with tobacco. 'I'm certainly going to take a look at them the first chance I get. What the devil does he mean by creeping up on me like that? I nearly jumped ten feet in the air when he switched his torch on. I didn't hear a sound, and before I knew it there I was, spotlighted like a ruddy crooner at the Palladium.'

I started lighting my pipe, feeling thoroughly annoyed.

She looked at me silently while I exhausted two matches.

'Do you think they're — alright?' she said. She looked a little upset. 'I mean . . . '

I shook my head, firmly, and used up a third match, but I wasn't feeling too happy. The small worm of unease that had made itself felt in the garden was still persisting, and I couldn't shake off the impression that his — or somebody's — eyes had made on me.

The pipe refused to behave itself and my wife was obviously a bit upset about the whole affair, so we listened to the radio for a bit and went to bed early.

It took me quite a while to get off to sleep, an unusual state of affairs, and she was still stirring restlessly when I dozed off. Also, I had a bit of a nightmare, another unusual event: a frighteningly pointless affair in which I was completely surrounded by gigantic searchlights that poured a glaringly concentrated pool of searing white light that nearly blinded me. And even as I clapped my hands over my eyes, I caught a vague impression of something lancing at me from the surrounding blackness, travelling with frightening velocity and ready to pin me in the circle of light like a butterfly on a collector's pad . . .

I woke, sweating profusely, just before it hit.

I was more than a little relieved when the alarm clattered and we had an excuse to get up.

★   ★   ★

Nothing at all happened during the next couple of days, at least as far as I was concerned. My wife reported that she'd seen them in the garden at odd intervals, and once they walked past the house while she was out at the front picking flowers. She'd said good-morning, but the only response she got was a brace of glances: one piercing, the other piscine. I didn't even catch a glimpse of them myself, but young David let it drop at breakfast that he'd seen them watching him from one of the upstairs windows as he left to catch the school bus in the mornings.

'And when I came home yesterday afternoon,' he said. He started tucking into his cornflakes with childish unconcern. My wife and I exchanged glances, but said nothing. I didn't like it, but there didn't seem to be anything we could do. People have a perfect right to look at who they please, especially from their own house. What the devil they were doing in one of the bedrooms at five o'clock in the afternoon I couldn't imagine, but then again, it was their concern. I swallowed the last of my breakfast, patted the boy on the shoulder, kissed my wife, and went out for the bus.

While I was passing the next house, I sneaked a look up at the upstairs windows. A curtain stirred briefly, then stilled. I caught a vague glimpse of a white face that moved suddenly backwards and was gone.

I felt a momentary twinge of fear. For a

split second I considered going back home, but the absurdity of it all kept me moving in the same direction. After all, the boy would be out, and I was perfectly confident that my wife was capable of looking after herself. I caught the bus, exchanged the usual polite greetings with my fellow travellers and went on to work, but I spent a pretty uneasy day. For the first time I found myself regretting that we didn't have a phone at the house. Before, we'd always considered ourselves fortunate that we were so completely cut off from outside communication, but now I wasn't so sure that it was such an advantage after all.

It was a distinct relief when five-thirty came around. I bade a hurried good-night to the caretaker, and practically raced to the bus stop. Not that anything was gained by rushing, but I had the absurd fear that, for once in its lethargic travels, the bus would be early and leave without me.

It was five past six when I turned the last bend in the road that led to the house. I had a good look at the house next door as I passed, but this time no curtains moved and no white face was apparent. Nevertheless, I hurried down the drive, almost at a jogtrot.

I heard the boy crying even before I opened the back door. I was in a cold sweat as I rushed in. The cause of the crying could have been anything: a cut knee, a bumped head, any one of a thousand minor accidents that youngsters are so prone to; but somehow this sound was different. A frightened crying, the sound of a child who had been subjected to something he doesn't understand.

I blundered into the kitchen, and stopped.

The boy was sitting at the table, his head cradled on his arms. My wife was kneeling by him, stroking his hair, patting his shoulder, in a vain attempt to soothe the muffled, racking sobs that came from him. She jumped as I came in, and got to her feet quickly. Her face was paper-white, and her eyes wide and frightened.

'Oh, thank *God* you're home!' she said. She seemed to crumple a little as she came over to me. She held my arm, and took a deep, shaking breath. She was never a heavy woman, but now she seemed drawn and shrunken to the point of emaciation. 'Those men . . . '

'Next door?' I said. I felt sick, and I was more frightened than I had ever been. I took her by the shoulders and peered at her with eyes that must have been as fear-ridden as her own. 'Well, *tell* me, for pity's sake! What's happened? What have they . . . ?'

'They met David on his way home from school,' she said. She seemed suddenly very tired. Her voice was quiet and lifeless. 'He met them at the top of the road. The tall one said good afternoon, and told David they were our new neighbours. David said, yes, he knew, and started to walk off. The tall one stopped him, and told him it wasn't very polite for someone to walk away just after they'd been introduced.' She looked as if she was going to cry. 'He asked David if he'd mind walking down the road with them, just for the talk. He said they didn't know anybody here, and they'd like to know about the people. What could the

63

boy do? He's been brought up to listen to his elders, and it only seemed polite . . . '

'But I've *told* him about things like that!' I said. I almost shouted. 'He's been told to keep away from strangers that want to talk to him! Good God, how many times . . . ?'

She shook her head, tiredly.

'He can't help it. He's just naturally friendly. And after all, we're always friendly to strangers, people that don't know their way about. It seems natural that he should be the same way . . . '

'But it's *not* the same!' I shouted. I was cold, but the sweat was running down my back in a steady stream. 'We're adults, we know what to do — !' I choked off. 'What happened?'

'The tall one talked. He asked David questions . . . '

'Questions?' I looked wildly at the boy, and then back to my wife. 'What the devil kind of questions get *this* kind of result?' I went over to the boy, knelt by the table, and lifted him upright. He was huddled and tense. His eyes were dreadfully red and swollen and he was still crying.

'David, son, tell me what happened.'

He told me. About the questions, and his answers that had seemed entirely automatic, as though the bright, burning eyes of the tall man had dragged them out of him against his will; about the dark, whispered suggestions that had kept him rooted like a rabbit before a stoat, as they stood in the lane where they had somehow wandered; and all the time the cold-fish glare of the silent sandman watching him with wet-lipped anticipation, his hands forever clenching and unclenching with a barely-controlled venom.

I knelt there, listening, and shaking like a tree in a high and terrible wind.

'And then I ran!' the boy cried. Earlier, his sobs had quieted a little, but now his face was crumpled into a puckered red mask of fear. 'He shouted at me to stop, but I ran and ran until I got here!' He tore himself out of my hands and threw himself face-downwards again. His muffled voice came from the shelter of his thin arms, and a small hand beat the table once in a gesture of frustrated, childish fear. 'He hated me! They *both* did! They *hated* me, and wanted me *dead!*'

Anger is a terrible thing. In the space of seconds it can turn a peaceful being into a thing of blood and wrath, obsessed with nothing but the desire to maim, tear and crush the thing that has caused his anger to swell from the dark depths where it lies, hidden and forever waiting. As I pushed myself upright and stood by the table, sick and shaking, I wanted blood. I wanted the blood of these prowling things next door, these dark and menacing creatures who had erupted into our lives, and in a space of days caused us to live in fear.

For a moment, I thought of the police, but I dismissed the idea. This was different, a private thing. I turned, and headed for the back door. My wife caught at my arm as I passed and tugged at me, fearfully.

'What are you going to do . . . ?'

I patted her hand and detached it, gently but firmly. I didn't look at her. I moved towards the door again.

'No!' Her voice was a high, frightened whisper. 'No, you mustn't . . . '

I went out, shutting the door behind me.

I went down the drive, out into the road, and turned into the gateway of the house next door. I caught a glimpse of movement in the front room, a flicker of the curtains, and then nothing.

I jammed my thumb against the bell and kept it there.

The door was answered sooner than I expected. About ten seconds after I commenced my onslaught of ringing, there was the click of the latch, and the door swung inwards.

It was the tall one, and for the first time I got a proper look at him. He was pale and thin, his clothing a nondescript grey suit, almost black. His forehead was high and protruding, and his face long and drawn. It was high-cheekboned, and with the long upper lip that so often indicates a superior intelligence. It was a striking face in itself, but dominated completely by the glowing, coal-like eyes that shone from beneath the heavy forehead, the eyes of someone consumed by a turbulently frightening inner fire.

In spite of myself, and the unabated tumult that beat inside my senses, I hesitated.

'We were expecting you,' he said. His eyes were fixed unblinkingly on mine, and there was a faintly malicious edge to his voice as he spoke. He sounded almost triumphant. 'Please come inside.'

'What I have to say can be said perfectly well where we — '

'I must insist that you come inside.' It was a lip-licking, anticipatory voice. 'What we have to say is not for the innocent ears of the birds and the flowers. It is better spoken behind closed doors, away from the cleanness of the open air and the normality of nature.' He stepped to one side. 'If you please.'

Despite my anger, despite my bubbling hatred of these men and their doings, the small flicker of fear made itself felt again. If anything, that was what I needed. I nodded, curtly, and walked into the hallway. The door clicked shut behind me.

He led the way down the passage to the rear of the house, opened a door and ushered me inside. His silent gesture was contemptuous. Clenching my teeth to control the anger that came surging to the surface even stronger than before, I stalked inside.

I stopped.

The small man sat in a far corner, his feet placed neatly side by side on the floor, his left hand resting docilely on his knee. In his right hand, the point towards me, he held a foot-long knife with a strange twisted blade.

I whirled. The tall man was closing the door, his back towards me. There was a double click, a slight fumbling motion, and then he turned.

The gun in his hand was as steady as a rock and pointed directly at me.

We stood for several seconds, just staring at one another. One thing was certain, he came out of that battle of the eyes the winner. In the space of a second, fear was the dominating sensation that gripped me. An icy hand traced its way down my spine, and I knew with an absolute, chilling certainty that these men were capable of killing me.

'What's this all about?' I said. My voice

was hoarse, and my remark sounded as foolish as my opening one at our first encounter over the garden fence. I could feel the dead-fish stare of the small man drilling icily into my back. I didn't move. 'Before we commence this conversation . . . '

'Before we commence any conversation,' said the tall man, 'you will sit down. Over there.' His eyes were bright with a terrible sadistic triumph. He gestured towards an easy chair set against the wall. We continued the exchange of glances while I complied, the gun turning in a slow, steady arc, following my progress like a menacing metallic shadow. I sat down on the edge of the chair.

'Back,' he said. He waved the gun, gently. 'Sit back.'

I leaned back, cursing silently. The small man was on my right, and while my chances of jumping the tall one successfully were virtually nil, they were now rendered doubly so by the treacherously springy upholstery that now encased me. I sank and waited, trying to control my shaking.

The tall one took his time about speaking, studying me first with those mad, luminescent pools for the best part of a minute. Beside me, the small man made no sound. I couldn't even hear him breathing. For all I knew, he could have been dead.

At last the tall one broke the tortuous, nerve-grinding silence.

'I spoke to your little boy today,' he said. 'An interesting conversation.' He seemed to relax a little, but the gun never wavered in his hand. He was smiling, a dreadful contraction of the facial muscles that never reached his eyes. 'A polite, well-mannered boy. Perhaps too well-mannered. If he had not been brought up with such a conventional respect for his elders and their whims, you would not be here now.'

'But I am here,' I said. My voice sounded like a rasping file. 'Why?'

The dreadful smile continued.

'Naturally, you questioned your son about our conversation. If he answered you truthfully, then you know that we expressed considerable interest in your occupation.' He licked his lips, carefully. 'You are, I understand, the mortician for the nearby town of Morley Park and the surrounding district.'

I nodded, slowly.

'That is true . . . '

'And as such, you are in sole charge of the local mortuary.' He licked his lips again. His eyes were bright and burning on my face. 'Is that correct?'

'There is a caretaker . . . '

'Who only deputises in your absence. Correct again?' He nodded, gently. 'Yes, I think so.' The smile was triumphant now, the smile of someone who is utterly sure of his ground and the direction it will take him if he follows it unquestioningly. His tongue ran over his lips as he savoured the next question, taking his time about the asking, relishing his certain fore-knowledge of the answer.

'And naturally a man in your position would have access to the building at all times. You have keys, for example?'

The sweat was pouring out of my cold skin in a steady stream. For the life of me I couldn't control my shaking. 'Of course . . . '

'Perhaps you have them with you now?' For one blindingly terrifying moment I caught a mental glimpse of myself at my place of work, only now my position was dreadfully, irrevocably changed. I was on one of the veined marble slabs, a naked, cold cadaver, motionless in the dim shrouded silence of the vault. And bending over me, the light from his insane eyes etching sharp black shadows across my dead and staring face, was the creature that stood opposite me in this musty, unaired room, staring at me with those same maniacal eyes and holding certain death in his hand.

'Yes . . . ' I said. My mouth was a dry, arid desert. The muscles around it were numb and frozen. I opened it with difficulty. 'Yes, I always carry them . . . '

'You must die now,' he said. It was so sudden, so horribly unexpected at that moment that for an instant what he'd said didn't register on my already half-fainting mind. His face was a dead, cold mask, his eyes with their dreadful burning light the only sign of life. 'In some ways I regret that it must be so soon and so final — however, we have a little something prepared in the cellar for your wife and boy . . . '

I almost fainted.

'My wife . . . '

'They must die, too.' His voice was a dim, toneless drumming in my ears. 'To kill only one of you would be useless. There must be no witnesses, no bearers of descriptions to those who would seek your killers . . . '

His eyes burned madly at me, and he talked on.

It was then or never, I knew. Then or never was my one pitifully absurd, impossible chance for life. It was what he'd said about the wife and boy that did it. If it hadn't been for that I think I might have sat there, a frozen corpse even before the bullet hit me, but that statement, so much more than just a threat, filled me with the kind of insane recklessness that results inevitably in either corpses or heroes.

I got a tight grip on the arms of the chair, and heaved.

I thank God now for several things. One is the fact that the chair was backed tight against the wall, his obvious aim being to have as much space as possible between us. The room, however, wasn't really large enough to make that really worthwhile, and the amount of solid leverage that I was able to obtain from it more than compensated from my point of view. Second, and something that at first glance might seem a doubtful advantage, I slipped and fell. The blessing there was that he'd been expecting me to come at him a little higher up, probably to try and grab the gun. Third was the fact that, while the little man was up and out of his chair like a streak of greased lightning, lunging at me as he came, he moved slightly behind me as he did so. He hadn't made a sound during our brief association, and he was incapable of making one after that.

The one bullet that the tall man fired whined over my back and took him just below the hairline. I lurched forward across the carpet as the tall man hesitated for one brief, dumbstruck second, wrapped my arms around his legs, and heaved. He wasn't a heavy man, despite his height. He toppled over backwards, and his head hit the wall with a dull crunching noise.

I heaved myself up and sprang astride

him, pinning his gun arm under my knee and twisting it hard with both hands. He moaned and let go, but his left arm was still free, his clawing hand seeking my eyes. His eyes were still glazed, but getting brighter by the second. I felt the strength in his body squirming back to life beneath me, and something gave in my mind.

It had to be done. It had been a long time, many long months, since I had done this thing to a living, breathing human, but it was the only way. I forced his free arm under my knee and bent towards the suddenly insanely frightened face.

And as I sank my teeth into his neck, cutting off the bubbling scream, I knew that this way — our way — was the only one . . .

★   ★   ★

The bundle of sharpened stakes that I found down in the cellar made quite a nice bonfire, together with several other items of interest that I found on the bodies. Notably, their identification. A card in the wallet of the tall one labelled him as A.

Hunter — a singularly appropriate name and not, I suspect, his own — and named him a member of a group that called themselves the Supernatural Slayers. I'd heard of it vaguely through other members of the family, but this was my first direct contact with any of its members.

The dagger was an interesting item. The twisted blade was teak, extremely effective I should imagine, and of the type found protruding from my Uncle George when his travels ended abruptly in a remote part of Asia. The dagger, the guns, and a spare box of silver bullets I buried with the bodies, alongside the corpse of old Broom, our previous neighbour; well away from the houses, and in a spot that was unlikely to receive agricultural attention for some considerable time.

Between us, my wife and I cooked up a yarn to spin to the house-agents and any other nosey-parkers that might consider it their business, including the police, but this time I have my doubts as to its success. It's a little complicated, involving a friend in a motor car who had rushed down from Leeds in a frightful hurry because the brother of the tall one was dangerously ill, and they hadn't had time to bring back the keys and rent in lieu of notice, and now they'd asked us to do it for them, going off in such a terrific tear that they hadn't even had time to write a note and leave an address for forwarding mail . . .

Hmm. I must confess, it does sound a bit thin. The police were very polite about it all, but my wife and boy have reported that they are being subjected to considerable scrutiny every time they go anywhere near the town. People who previously greeted me and seemed willing to indulge in a certain amount of conversation now find sudden and urgent business waiting for them on the other side of the street whenever I approach.

Perhaps it would be best if we were to consider a change of address in the near future. Jobs, of course, are a difficulty, particularly those offering the amenities of my present one — I wonder, under the circumstances, if a family member who might possibly be reading this could help me in the matter.

It would be greatly appreciated.

The Devil and
Mr. Wooller

'I wonder,' asked Mr. Wooller, 'if I might trouble you for a match.'

The Devil murmured politely, fumbled in the pockets of his light topcoat, produced a box of Swan Vestas, and proffered them. His eyes were completely devoid of curiosity.

Mr. Wooller's hands shook as he held them cupped over the tip of his cigarette, but he felt that he could be excused this slight outlet to his excitement. Most people, on finding the Devil standing next to them at Waterloo station, would doubtless have screamed, fainted, taken to their heels, or possibly even expired. None of these occurred to Mr. Wooller, to whom the Devil was now a regrettably familiar figure.

'I shouldn't be doing this,' he said.

The Devil raised his eyebrows.

'Smoking,' explained Mr. Wooller, and coughed gently a couple of times, without removing the cigarette from his mouth. 'Had my tonsils out a few weeks ago, and you know what that's like at my age. Took it out of me, in more ways than one, I don't mind saying.'

The Devil nodded, sympathetically.

'Been staying with my sister down at Brighton for the week,' said Mr. Wooller. 'Could've stayed longer, but she's got enough to do without pampering an invalid like me.' He scratched the back of his neck, and felt the gun sag a little lower in his raincoat pocket. 'Besides, I'll have to be getting back on the job sooner or later.'

Mr. Wooller puffed jerkily, and then removed the cigarette from his mouth.

'Commercial travel's a bigger hustle these days than it used to be. Do you,' asked Mr. Wooller, greatly daring, and fixedly eyeing a slot machine on the opposite platform, 'do much travelling yourself?'

The Devil smiled.

'A great deal,' he said. His voice was deep and not unpleasant. 'My vocation requires me to be in a great many places in the course of a year. But travel is, after all, very conducive — ' He eyed Mr. Wooller in a friendly way. ' — to a broadening of the mind.'

Mr. Wooller shuddered. He was suddenly recalling his own initial encounter with this long, lean, and frighteningly bland world traveller.

The printing trade of the small Midland town had been booming, and correspondingly the demand for printing inks and paper had been large. Mr. Wooller, his order book comfortably full, had been standing on the pavement edge only a few yards away from her, when the little girl in the scarlet coat was lifted as though by strings and bowled beneath the rampaging wheels of a lorry that lurched suddenly round the corner.

He heard the screech of metal on metal as the green street-corner lamp suffered a warping blow, and the death-rattle of the small corner house as its bricks cascaded at absurd angles; he saw the flames that leaped thunderously skywards, and all his half-born heroism died as he flung himself flat in the dusty garden of the house in front of which he was standing, cursing the absurdly low wall that separated the property from the street.

After the explosion, numbed, deafened, and blinded by dust, Mr. Wooller rose stumblingly to his feet and ran around the fantastically-blazing piles of bricks and masonry towards the dead and dying people. He tried to help when panic-stricken householders clutched at his sleeve and begged his assistance in removing belongings to a place of safety; but something was troubling him, and it had nothing to do with his prudent leap behind the wall when instinctive common sense had told him plainly that it was the one sane move he could have made.

Suddenly Mr. Wooller felt evil around him, and its dark and pungent presence was very frightening. Between the oily columns of smoke the sky showed blue and clear, yet to him the street was dark with more than merely smoke and sinless death. It was while he was helping to carry a cumbersome, marble-topped washstand towards the growing collection of settees, bedsteads, and gilt-framed pictures, that he first saw him.

The Devil was standing at the back of a rapidly-filling gap in the crowd of onlookers, and appeared, oddly enough, to be causing no stir among those nearest to him. His hat was dark, adorned with a small red feather in the band, and his topcoat was light and of an excellent cut. No horns or spiked tail were in evidence before the crowd surged across Mr. Wooller's point of vision, but the spear-point moustache and Van Dyke beard were as near to his wildest nightmares, and twitching with a sardonic impudence that could only be described as devilish.

Mr. Wooller stumbled, and his end of the washstand scraped along the pavement.

'What the — ' said the man in front.

'There,' choked Mr. Wooller. He was sweating violently, and his pointing hand trembled. 'There, at the back of the crowd. I just saw . . . '

'Look, mate,' said the man ahead of him. His home was burning to a cinder, and he felt no inclination to stop and argue with Mr. Wooller. 'If there's somebody over there you want to 'ave a yarn with, don't let me 'old yer back. But somebody's got to 'elp me shift this stuff, and we're not gettin' far at this rate. Charlie!' He ignored Mr. Wooller. 'Come and give us a lift with this thing. Seems our friend-in-need 'ere . . . '

But Mr. Wooller had gone, edging his way desperately through the tight ranks of people. He was breathing hard and shaking dreadfully with the appalling absurdity of it all, but he never for one moment doubted either his sanity or the efficiency of his eyesight. He had seen Mephistopheles, gazing with dark and triumphant eyes at a deed of his doing that would hereafter be spoken of as an accident — a sad and terrible freak affair, brought about by the carelessness of a little girl who had started to cross the road without first looking both ways.

Mr. Wooller arrived, panting, at the back of the crowd, with the picture of the child hurtling through the air, propelled by no earthly force, still hauntingly clear in his mind. The Devil had gone. In his place stood a short, stocky man in a cloth cap and muffler, a racing paper beneath his arm, and an empty pipe between his teeth. He answered Mr. Wooller's stare with an openly hostile look.

The street was free of devils. Even as he stared dumbly about him, the oppressing darkness that only he seemed to see suddenly lifted. No trace of the Devil remained, and Mr. Wooller, seating himself on the nearest kerbstone, allowed himself to be suddenly and violently sick.

The second occasion had been a little different.

A mild political discussion between two navvies in the bar of a public house in Hackney, where Mr. Wooller chanced to be lunching, had suddenly, and for no apparent reason, developed into a blasphemous row the like of which he had never witnessed before, even in his army days. Steadily, and with an awful deliberateness that seemed beyond their power to control, the two big men had whipped themselves into mutual states of homicidal unreasonableness.

Mr. Wooller, a little frightened, decided

to get out before any blows were actually struck. He was fumbling stealthily beneath his chair for his briefcase when he saw the figure in the window-seat and paused, as though suddenly and miraculously carved out of stone.

There was no mistaking that dark hat, and light and expensive topcoat. The trim moustache was even neater than before, but it was the Devil as he had first seen him, only now he was fastidiously consuming bread and cheese, a beer tankard at his elbow. As Mr. Wooller heard the first jarring blow from the direction of the bar, the Devil nicked a crumb from the corner of his mouth with an inappropriately white handkerchief, rose to his feet, and passed quietly from the building.

One of the navvies died. The other was so badly cut about — they had quickly resorted to the use of shattered beer mugs — that it was a wonder he survived to go for trial. Mr. Wooller was a witness for the prosecution, but what could he say? Could he state, under oath, that he had seen a murder promoted by the Devil actually committed under the eyes of its instigator?

Mr. Wooller had no wish to go to a lunatic asylum. He committed perjury, and passed from the courtroom a respected and truthful witness to all those present, and a miserable and tortured being with a freak trick of observance to himself.

When he arrived back at his lodgings on the final day of the trial, with the knowledge that Clement Fisher, the navvy, would shortly be hanged by the neck until he was dead, Mr. Wooller sank into the basket-chair by the window of his bedroom and stared unseeingly at the neat, peacefully-secure rows of rooftops that covered the neighbouring estate.

He was not a clever man. He shared the scepticism and doubts of the majority of his fellow men as far as a God in Heaven and a Devil in Hell were concerned, and was filled with a hopeful belief that the solution was as black and white as that; but he was nagged consistently by the boomingly confident voice of scientific reasoning. When his wife had been alive, he had attended Sunday services apathetically because she wished it: bored by the preachers, whose quotations and denunciations seemed unnecessarily riddled with italicised phrases; and subdued during the hymns, helped little by a singing voice that had maintained a constant tunelessness since childhood. Since her death, his half-hearted attendance had ceased altogether. Now, shatteringly, his doubts had been dispelled for him. A Devil existed.

Slowly, Mr. Wooller sat upright in his chair. He recalled the tankard of beer, the plate of bread and cheese. An internal system was needed to accommodate such earthly fare — a throat, a stomach, a liver, kidneys, a heart to pump the black and evil blood. When on earth, the Devil obviously assumed the bodily characteristics of man, and should surely be vulnerable to man's catastrophes. So reasoned Mr. Wooller, and as each thought was planted and took root in his mind, so the reasons for his extraordinary powers of observation were revealed to him.

He rose, crossed to the bureau, and

opened the middle drawer.

He took out the small brown box with the brass fastening that lay at the back beneath his shirts, unlocked it with the miniature brass key on his key-chain, and took out the gun.

It was a relic of the First World War, contained three bullets, and was in perfect working order. Once a year, on the anniversary of his demobilisation, Mr. Wooller removed it from its coverings, oiled it, worked the breech a few times, pointed it playfully at himself in the mirror, and replaced it in the box. For Mr. Wooller had always been an adventurer at heart, and although the only action he had witnessed had been at his desk behind the lines, no Second Lieutenant had been better prepared for conflict.

Now he weighed the gun lightly and thoughtfully in his hand, and placed it in his briefcase.

From that day he carried it, sometimes in the briefcase, and sometimes in the pocket of his raincoat. He had no licence, but he reasoned that such a formality was superfluous under the circumstances. If a man carried a revolver solely for the purpose of eliminating the Devil when next he encountered him, a legal triviality could surely be overlooked.

It was some months later that he had his tonsils removed. They had been slowly poisoning his system for some time past, and his work was suffering. Although his doctor had pointed out that it was a little late in life for the operation, he had decided to undergo the indignity of the knife; then, taking advantage of an open invitation, he had gone to stay with his sister at Brighton during his convalescent period. And it was while travelling back to London that he once again found himself in the Devil's presence.

Entering the restaurant car, his eye fastened on a hat and folded coat, resting on the rack above an aisle seat at the far end of the carriage. There was no mistaking them. Mr. Wooller's tongue clave to the roof of his mouth, and perspiration beaded his forehead. He wondered if he should dispense with all formalities, and there and then walk down the aisle and blow the Satanic brains all over the restaurant car; but then he remembered that the revolver was in his raincoat pocket in the compartment he had just left.

So he sank quietly into the nearest seat, and just as quietly ordered a double brandy. The Devil, clad in respectable light tweeds, finished his meal unmolested, flicked a crumb from the corner of his mouth with what looked like the same milk-white handkerchief he had used before, and retired, presumably to his own compartment.

At Waterloo, easily spotted by a dry-mouthed and shakily-determined Mr. Wooller, the Devil seemed in no hurry to leave the station. He strolled unhurriedly to another platform, halfway down which he paused, and retired to an elegantly lounging position against the nearest railings. Mr. Wooller, from his position behind a pile of luggage, noticed his quarry's steady interest in a group of men, soberly-clad, standing rather formally a few yards away.

His hand taut on the butt of the lethal

weapon in his pocket, Mr. Wooller hailed a passing porter.

'That bunch down there,' he said, nodding sideways and slipping a half-crown into the man's hand. 'Do you know who they are?'

Mr. Wooller was tingling with excitement. His own gaze, forever flickering between the Devil and the group of men, failed to see the dawning of suspicion in the porter's eyes.

'Reception committee,' said the man. He seemed suddenly anxious to be about his business. 'From one of the embassies. 'Scuse me, guv'nor, but I've got a load of luggage to shift.'

He was off before Mr. Wooller could question him further. So that was it, thought Mr. Wooller, and wriggled his shoulders a little as he felt the trickle of sweat down his spine. A full-blooded assassination. Somewhere in this crowd lurked a fanatic, armed with gun, bomb, or knife, ready to dispense death the moment the incoming diplomat stepped from the train.

There was no time for discreet questioning and the warning of officials.

That was when Mr. Wooller, making the most momentous decision of his life, had stuck an unlighted cigarette in the corner of his mouth, stepped from his hiding place and, strolling to where the Devil stood, politely asked him for a match . . .

Conversation, such as it had been, died, but Mr. Wooller had established his bridgehead. He stood there at the peak of his adventure, a middle-aged commercial traveller for a printing-ink manufacturer, rather shabby and more than a little afraid, clutching an old Webley in his raincoat pocket, and determined at all costs to forestall the deviltry that was scheduled for that day and place.

Sudden activity on the platform announced the approach of the train. A loudspeaker boomed. A fraction of a second before the stirring of the passengers on the platform commenced, the Devil started to move.

Slowly and majestically, he stepped forward — a true Prince of Darkness — towards the isolated group that had now stiffened into a semblance of attention.

Mr. Wooller, sweating profusely, followed a bare six feet behind.

The train slid grindingly to a halt.

There was a craning of necks among the group as a myriad doors disgorged people on to the platform, then a sudden sharp voice in a foreign tongue. The reception committee quickly and efficiently grouped itself into a flying wedge that brushed aside all opposition, then flowed smoothly into a half circle in front of a first-class carriage door.

The Devil walked straight towards them.

Mr. Wooller, horribly rattled, faltered for a split second, then he too plunged on. Surely the Devil himself would not . . . ? Mr. Wooller's eyes, stinging with the salt of his perspiration, frantically sought any movement in the crowd that would announce the assassin's position. He saw none.

The half circle of figures split suddenly into two facing lines, forming a short, narrow corridor. As the grey-bearded passenger with the dark features and the puckered brow strode forward between the ranks, the Devil halted and faced him, his hands sliding slowly from the pockets of his coat.

Mr. Wooller panicked.

In a frenzy of fear, he lurched forward, tearing his own gun from his pocket, his free hand fumbling wildly at the safety catch. He thrust the gun forward, jamming the barrel hard against the Satanic spinal column — and fired three times.

Voices rose in deafening tumult around him. Dazed, Mr. Wooller gazed upon the body of the man he had killed. He lay sprawled at the feet of his fellow-countrymen, a small, grey-bearded man from whose dark features all puckers had been miraculously erased, and whose overcoat now showed dark red stains.

Angry, brutal hands seized Mr. Wooller, and he was hurried without ceremony into a nearby office.

They were unkind enough to bring the body of the diplomat into the same room and rest it gently on the floor, directly opposite the corner where Mr. Wooller was savagely being bundled into a pair of handcuffs. When the police, after listening to the testimony of the porter and other less important witnesses, came to take him away, Mr. Wooller was still staring at the body with wild and reddened eyes, and sobbing brokenly to the grim-faced men around him, 'But didn't any of you see him, not any of you?'

They assured him, not unkindly, that they had not; and it was only as he was being led away that Mr. Wooller suddenly began to appreciate the amount of patient preparation and the really devilish cunning that had gone into it all.

The Other Man

With his back to the window he had broken, he stood listening to the faintly dusty silence in the cottage.

Gradually, he allowed himself to relax. There was no-one here, he was now quite sure. Even if there were a bedridden occupant who had chosen to ignore his earlier use of the front-door knocker, his eventual entry would at least have provoked some sort of query by this time.

He looked about him. The room in which he stood was a kitchen, its walls white and carrying no decoration. There were three doors, two panelled and the third a lighter affair that obviously led to a pantry. The table and four wooden chairs were plain waxed wood, and a recess beside the pantry door contained a small stove, with a gas bottle leaning in the corner.

He glanced over his shoulder through the window, carefully studying the sunlit clutter of the woods and the tire-rutted dirt road beyond the white fence that enclosed the untended garden behind the cottage; then he moved across the kitchen to the nearer panelled door and opened it.

It led directly into the living room, a surprisingly large room that must at one time have been two smaller ones. A staircase was on his right, and the front door of the cottage was directly in front of him. He crossed the living room to the nearest window and moved the closed curtain fractionally to one side. Glances in both directions reassured him that the path he had left little more than a minute before was still deserted, an empty strip of baked earth that curved gently beside the placid sheen of the river.

He wandered about the room, studying its contents. These walls were also white, but this time they carried simply-framed reproductions of paintings. With a start of pleasure he saw that one of them was a Rousseau, a personal favourite — a thing of sombre greens and one patch of sullen red, a scene of shadowed violence that had gripped his imagination ever since he had first seen it in a museum.

He looked at the other pictures. There were a Klee and a Shahn, the Klee only vaguely familiar, but the Shahn one that he remembered clearly — the violinist in his dark and formal suit contrasting sharply with the rural dress and simple instruments of his fellow musicians.

He brushed a hand absently at the dusty front of his overalls and looked thoughtfully at the rest of the room. The furniture was a carefully-chosen blending of old and new — modern lounge chairs contrasting pleasantly with the more traditionally-styled items. There was a recess on each side of the open fireplace: one with unpainted shelving filled with books, the other containing a cabinet with a portable record player on top of it. He went over to the cabinet, knelt, and slid the doors back. One compartment contained glasses and bottles, the other long-playing records.

He reached for a bottle, uncorked it, and tilted it against his mouth. The whiskey fumes, unfamiliar after so long a time, caught at his throat. He coughed, corked the bottle, placed it on top of the cabinet, then reached inside the second compartment and pulled out the top record.

He read the bold type on the cover with a cautiously wondering look, his pose suddenly one of disbelieving wariness. Placing the record beside the bottle, he reached for others, extracting a few this time. He flipped through them with a kind of numbed fascination, hungrily identifying them. Then he spread them in a neat semicircle around him, muttering names in a barely audible voice.

Stravinsky, Ellington, Bartøk, Ravel, Armstrong, Parker, Holst, Basie. He rested a hand that shook slightly on the nearest cover. It was firm to his touch, a tangible link with things he had once had and lost, and their loss was now suddenly more terrible than it had ever been, a knife of memories that dug deep into his mind.

He rose and moved aimlessly about the room, touching things with nervous fingertips. Despite their reassuring solidity he returned to each item several times, now smoothing or gripping it; as though afraid that each was a fragment of a mirage that would fade and vanish unless he repeatedly obtained tactile and irrefutable evidence of its reality.

At last he paused and found himself looking directly at the bookshelves. He stared at them for some time without moving. Something, he knew, had pulled him past them during his circuit of the room, so that in fact he had not touched them once or even glanced closely at them. He absently acknowledged this, and also the inescapable fact that this omission had been occasioned by sheer funk; a fear that what he might find there would in some way disturb the pattern that was gradually resolving around him.

'Thurber,' he said aloud. His voice was slightly hoarse. 'Waugh. Chandler. Wodehouse.' He paused and laughed, nervously. 'Bradbury.'

Kneeling, he ran his eyes slowly across each shelf, savouring familiar titles like a gourmet who had long been denied food that would genuinely excite his palate. They were all there, sandwiched between tantalisingly-unread authors and titles: some of whom he knew vaguely by name, others that were totally unfamiliar.

He fumbled one of these from the shelf and glanced at the contents page. It was a science-fiction anthology, its stories striking chords of varying resonance in his memory.

He replaced it carefully, let his eyes wander hungrily along the other shelves, nodding frequently as though acknowledging the presence of old friends.

After a time he rose and crossed the room to the stairs, still moving cautiously, but with an undercurrent of elation that now added briskness to his walk.

He found a solitary bedroom at the top of the house: a long, low-ceilinged room that contained a double bed, modern unmatched chairs, and a dressing table with a smudge of face powder on its top. There was a curtained alcove at the far end, empty except for a few wire clothes-hangers. He moved back to the bed and tested it with both hands, smiling at the softly-sprung reaction that he felt.

He went downstairs again, through the

living room and into the kitchen. One of the panelled doors yielded a toilet. Behind the pantry door he saw a handful of cans and bottles — meatloaf, peas, beans, soup, apricots, and condensed milk. One of the bottles contained instant coffee. He walked slowly back into the living room and slumped in a chair, tilting his head back and closing his eyes.

The picture was now clear. This was a weekend cottage, the property of a man whose tastes matched his own to an almost uncanny degree, even to the style of decor and furnishings. A successful man, who possessed enough money to create a sanctuary where he could temporarily escape his work and responsibilities, lulled by the restful quiet of the surroundings and the books and music of his choice.

A man like himself in many ways — but with one irremovable difference.

He grimaced, and moved restlessly in his chair. It was almost as though his discovery of this place was a piece of sadistically-calculated punishment, a cruel and deliberate demonstration of what might have been. But he had blundered, and the last five months, surrounded by bleak grey stone and whitewashed walls, had been the price of his greed and stupidity.

Now these things were forever beyond attainment, dreams that would torment him for a while and then inevitably fade and die in the furtive future of running and hiding that confronted him, never knowing when an authoritative hand would seize his shoulder or a uniformed figure block his path.

He swore, a sudden burst of directionless invective, and opened his eyes. Sunlight was cutting a swathe down the wall in front of him, ending dazzlingly on the polished wooden top of a small gate-leg table.

In the centre of this almost blinding brightness was a framed photograph that he had somehow bypassed during his earlier exploration of the room.

He stared at it without moving, slitting his eyes against the glare, sullenly reluctant despite his burning curiosity to confront what he assumed to be a portrait of his unwitting host. Then reasoning doubt tempered his initial flush of animosity.

Would such a person be likely to keep a

photograph of himself? He queried his own streak of narcissism, and found the answer to be a firm negative. Pushing himself out of the chair, he crossed the room and looked down at the portrait.

It was a photograph of a woman in a sweater and skirt, with a large kerchief on her head, knotted beneath her chin. Fair hair showed in a careless fringe that covered part of her forehead. She was leaning against a stone wall, her feet crossed, and she was laughing. He judged her to be a little younger than his own twenty-seven years. He picked up the frame, walked back to the chair and sank into it, holding the picture in front of him with both hands.

It was a good photograph, the details sharp and clear. The two rings on her left hand showed plainly the carelessly displayed badges of respectability and ownership. He stared woodenly, his mouth hot and dry. Here, then, was the ultimate seal of triumph, the possession of a beautiful woman; one who could love such a man, sharing his tastes and desires, the partner who slept with him in the bed upstairs. A woman who might, in other times and other circumstances, have been his.

His mind slid dully back to his own amours: a spasmodic series of shallow and unresolved relationships that had all concluded flatly, their collective aftertaste more one of relief than misery. He had always been finicky about women, consciously seeking one with whom he could experience genuine rapport, a true partner whom he could turn to with the knowledge that his emotions were shared; but his idealistic search had been fruitless, inevitably terminating in cul-de-sacs of misunderstanding or boredom.

But this must be such a woman. He stared at the laughing face and trim figure in the photograph, a hard lump of futility lodged tightly in his throat.

He rose again, tiredly, and replaced the frame on the table, then wandered back into the kitchen. Common sense nudged at his apathy, telling him that he must eat — he had had no food for over twenty-four hours — and then decide on his next move. The cottage was a temporary refuge only, a place of blessed shelter that he had been fortunate to find; but the prison from which he had escaped was a bare twenty miles away, and isolated houses such this would inevitably be included in the ever-widening net that the authorities would have spread by now.

It was only in a city that he could hope for permanent freedom, some large anonymous place where money, which he would have to steal, would buy the means of getting him out of the country. As he saw it, he had no other choice. His attempt to rob his employers had been a solitary affair, and his parents' reaction at the time of his arrest and imprisonment had left him with no illusions that help of any kind could be expected from that quarter. None of his friends possessed enough money; and he wryly conceded that, even if they did, not a single one of them could be trusted not to salvage his conscience and respectability by turning him in.

He took some cans from the pantry and opened them. The bottle of gas, he found, was half-full. He lit the stove and made coffee, swallowing the hot and bitter fluid greedily between spooned mouthfuls of beans as he sat at the kitchen table, his mind drifting greyly back over the events that had brought him to this sanctuary.

At first, almost numbed by his sense of guilt, he had not found prison the total nightmare he had expected. But as time dissipated this protective coating he had begun to view his surroundings with a queasy sense of horror, gradually aware of the vast gulf that separated him from the majority of its occupants.

There were others like himself: a handful of withdrawn, quiet men whose solitary falls from grace had similarly led to apprehension and punishment; but they formed a small segment of the prison's population. For the most part, the men with whom he worked, ate, and shared sleeping quarters were practised criminals, the possessors of an inverted code of ethics that he found wholly terrifying.

His escape he genuinely considered to have been a natural consequence of his awareness, an evolutionary step in his existence that had become as necessary as air and water. It had been traditional in procedure and surprisingly easy: a sudden pall of mist had permitted him to simply walk away from the working gang of which he was a member, and then circle around it to head north instead of the to-be-expected eastern route to the towns and cities.

An aimless period of skulking flight had followed, an exhausting passage of time that had at last brought him to the woods, and eventually to this cottage.

He finished eating, carefully washed the utensils, and replaced them where he had found them. He returned to the living room and once again lay back in the chair, some of his tension now gone.

He closed his eyes, deliberately shutting out the photograph; reluctant to do so but realizing that its distraction would only aggravate his maudlin thoughts.

Drowsily, he tried to marshal his limited knowledge of the neighbourhood, the location of roads and towns, but his thoughts persistently returned to his immediate surroundings and the strange pattern of coincidence that had brought him there.

He knew he must leave, that to stay meant an inevitable magnification of his personal danger; but the world outside, unfamiliar and inhabited by a menacing multiplicity of people and things, both horrified and repelled him.

The walls of the cottage and what they contained, this chair in which he sat, were safe refuges against these terrors.

Gradually his head lolled and his breathing deepened. One arm slid down slowly and limply beside the chair . . .

It was dusk when he woke. He shivered involuntarily and blinked at the shadowed room, fuzzily reorienting himself; unwilling to leave the comforting blankness of his sleep, but already experiencing again the strange sense of compatibility that he shared with his surroundings.

It was very quiet, with only faint insect sounds disturbing the orange-tinted silence outside. He pushed himself to his feet and padded to the kitchen, drank deeply from the cold-water tap, then returned to stand in the centre of the living room.

In the dim light, the photograph was an enigmatic patch of shadow now barely visible. He stared at it, watching it gradually merge with the deeper shadows until at last it seemed to vanish.

The room was almost dark when he moved forward, his hands outstretched before him. They found the invisible indentations of the frame, and he fumbled it hungrily from the table, staring down at the featureless wedge of blackness between his hands, the gloom somehow assuaging the turmoil of emotions that bit like acid into his body and mind.

Stiffly, and with his head bowed, he groped his way up the stairs, sprawling exhaustedly on the bed, the glass that covered the picture smoothly cold beneath one outstretched palm . . .

★　★　★

The sun was high when he finally rolled onto his back and opened his eyes again. He stared at the low ceiling, listening to the sharp birdcalls that occasionally cracked the warm silence of the woods; he was reluctant to move, but knew he must.

He shifted restlessly against the covers. Must? Why *must* he? Where could he find another shelter that in any way compared with his present one, where he would find refuge, food, and a bed? He thought of the books and records downstairs, a sudden hunger for just the sight of them tugging at his mind.

Why not stay for a day or two more, until the food was gone and he was forced to move on? By then the search would probably have passed him by, moving further past towards the more heavily populated areas. Surely it was at least possible that the cottage might be overlooked . . .

He jerked himself up off the bed in one convulsive movement, cursing at the wheedling voice in his mind. This was simply an extension of the dream; a tenuous, futile hope that somehow the existence of the house would be removed from the consciousness of the people searching for him, so that they would flow out and around the spot where it stood, carelessly passing it by as they would a rock or a tree.

He paced feverishly about the room, willing himself away from this lassitude that a cold and prickling corner of his mind told him he must cast out now, before it was too late. The cottage, he realized, was in its own way becoming another prison, a padded snare where, unless he moved on, he would cower until the inevitable time of discovery — if not by the police, then some passer-by, or even the owners.

He stood stock-still, staring at the crumpled covers on the bed. The photograph lay partially covered by an overturned sheet, the glass dull and blank in the shadow it cast.

He moved slowly back to the bed and picked up the picture, staring down at it with suffering eyes, then with a muffled cry hurled it across the room. It struck the wall beside the stairs with a splintering crack and fell to the carpet, shards of glass surrounding the frame.

He went past it and down the stairs, moving quickly, trying by sheer speed of action to shut his mind against the clamour of anger and frustration that boiled inside him. He savagely rifled the pantry, carelessly stuffing cans into the pockets of his overalls, then a can opener and a knife. About to slam the table drawer closed in a final gesture of impotent fury, he suddenly froze.

Through the window he saw movement beyond the white fence. A man was walking there, a creel slung from his shoulder and a canvas-wrapped fishing rod in one hand.

He shrank back into the room, listening to the muffled, measured footsteps that unhurriedly approached; and then, mercifully, went on.

There was no break in their rhythm that he could detect, no hesitation to indicate that the window he had broken had been seen.

Moving silently, he went back into the living room and flattened himself beside a window. Through the slit beside the curtain, he saw the man moving away down the path, casually studying the surface of the water.

He relaxed gradually, taking in deep, shuddering breaths, appalled at the narrowness of his escape. If he had wakened one minute earlier and then followed the same pattern of action, by this time —

He smeared a shaking hand across his face, and moved quietly back across the room, suddenly feeling strangely calm.

It was as though his attempted departure and its conclusion had resolved his relationship with the cottage, relieving him of any further decision. Simply, his near-encounter with the fisherman meant that the woods were not the safely empty place he had assumed them to be, and he would plainly have to wait until cover of darkness before he could leave without fear of further such meetings.

He emptied his pockets, replacing their contents, then went back into the living room and up the stairs to the bedroom.

Kneeling, he picked up the photograph, carefully removing the remains of splintered glass inside the frame and collecting the pieces that littered the carpet.

He carried them downstairs, dumped the broken glass in a pail beneath the sink, then took the picture back into the living room and returned it to the table, repositioning it carefully before turning away with an air of tired finality.

A cedar-wood box on the mantelpiece that he had failed to examine before yielded a handful of cigarettes. He took one, lit it with a book match that lay beside the box, and drew the smoke deeply and luxuriously into his lungs, ducking his head at the faintly dizzy reaction that this caused. The tobacco was stale, but not too unpleasantly so.

He selected a book from the shelves, the science-fiction anthology he had picked out on the previous day, seated himself in one of the lounge chairs, and began to read.

He read unhurriedly for several hours. His absorption in the stories was complete, a period during which he was relaxed, cocooned in a kaleidoscope of other places and times, distant futures where men and other beings played out their destinies in bizarre and ingenious ways. He enjoyed the book enormously, as he had known he would.

He finished it and selected another, sprawling back in the chair again, glancing once at the photograph on the table before opening the book and recommencing reading.

When he became hungry, he went out to the kitchen and heated soup, completing the meal with canned meat and fruit. He cleaned the dishes again, lit another cigarette, and returned to the living room.

He read for a while, then placed the book on one side and rose to study the record player. It was battery-operated, and a faint hum replied to his pressing of the ON switch.

He selected a record from the cabinet, placed it on the turntable, and carefully lowered the arm and needle onto its rim. The impressionistic patterns of Ravel languorously filled the room, a blanket of gentle sound that pricked nostalgically at his mind. He reduced the volume to a little above a whisper, then sat down again, his eyes closed and his hands crossed loosely in his lap.

He spent the remainder of the afternoon alternately playing records and reading. Despite the streak of pragmatism that assured him of the true nature of the situation, he was immensely soothed, devouring the imaginative play of word and sound with the voracity of a starving man, as near to being at peace for the first time since — when? He couldn't remember.

His surroundings induced a sense of well-being that was unknown to him, a formula for serenity that he had never considered attainable and which, while he still saw it as an ingredient of some calculated trick of fate, he was at last able to accept without bitterness.

The light was beginning to fade when he finally rose, replaced the book, and stood looking at the slowly darkening room for the last time.

There was something fitting about this last sight of it, as though its gradually softening contours were deliberately dimming his memory, making his departure less of a wrench than if he had been able to see clearly.

Finally he looked at the photograph, once again a blurred and featureless shape, and he nodded to it, briefly expressing regret for what he had done and also for what might have been.

He went out to the kitchen and brewed coffee, staring through the window at the darkening tangle of the woods as he slowly drank, tentatively wondering which would be his safest route once he was in the clear.

He washed and replaced the cup and saucer and once again took cans from the pantry, unhurriedly selective now, then opened the table drawer and took out a spoon, a can opener, and lastly a knife.

Faintly, ever so faintly, a car engine sounded outside in the gathering dusk.

He stiffened, his hand clamped on the wooden handle of the knife, an icy coldness abruptly gripping his throat and stomach.

The sound was like a sudden violent blow, a thunderous buffet that crashed through the barrier of his tranquillity and savagely thrust him back into a world of shadows, a place where he could only run and hide, dwelling briefly in one patch of darkness before encroaching danger forced him to run and hide again, a compulsory and terrifying game that he must almost certainly lose.

Dry-mouthed and sick, he stood motionless beside the table as the sound grew steadily louder, faded, then coughed gently to a silence directly outside the cottage.

He heard the sound of a door opening, a muffled exchange of conversation, then a metallic slam. Footsteps came quickly towards the front of the cottage.

He moved then, numbly turning to face the open door that led into the living room. A detached part of his mind told him that one rapid movement would take him up onto the table against which he rigidly leaned, another would release the window catch, and a third take him outside to where he could leap the low fence and be immediately lost in the darkening woods.

He knew that it would take only seconds, but still he stood facing the doorway, staring fixedly through the shadowed living room at the dark patch of the front door.

Then, above the paralyzing thunder inside him, he heard the scrape of an inserted key and the faint click as it was turned.

The door opened.

For several seconds she failed to see him where he stood, statue-like, in the gloom of the kitchen. He saw her near-silhouette against the oblong of twilit trees, and then she was inside, setting down a small suitcase. Straightening, she paused, and in a flush of shame he knew that she had caught sight of the missing glass in the photograph frame.

She stood motionless for a second, then her head darted in rapid, searching movements. She froze again when she finally saw him, her sharp intake of breath a small explosion in the deep silence of the room.

He stepped forward, searching the shocked but still beautiful face with shy hunger, hoping to reassure her by unhurried movement, lifting his hands in a gently placatory way.

'It's all right,' he said. 'I'm not going to — ' He broke off in horror as the forgotten knife rose up before his eyes, its blade a flash of menace in the gloom. Then the woman screamed a name.

'John!' She backed a solitary step, then screamed again. 'John, *John!*'

He blundered to a halt, jerking the knife fretfully, shaking his head rapidly from side to side. 'No, no please — '

Outside there was a startled exclamation, the sound of something striking the ground, then a pounding of footsteps. A shadow bulked in the doorway, paused momentarily, then lunged towards him.

In the seconds before the man reached him, despite his terror he was conscious chiefly of a feeling of surprise. While he had never attempted to draw a picture in his mind of his emotional counterpart, he had assumed in a hazy and perhaps vain way that he bore at least a passing physical resemblance to himself.

But the figure before him was tall and solidly-built, contrasting sharply with his own slenderness; a dark and hugely handsome manifestation beyond his wildest imaginings.

Confronted by it, he quailed, feeling himself shrink to an awed and insignificant shadow that crouched spellbound, a rabbit before the magnetically freezing approach of a stoat.

The blow took him on the side of the face and he spun away from it, the knife still tightly in his fist, reeling back across the kitchen and colliding heavily with the table. A vice-like set of fingers gripped his shoulder and heaved him around. He stumbled and somehow broke free, and they confronted each other. He jerked the knife in front of him, sobbing.

And then he looked across the heavy shoulder, past the darkly handsome face that held its own shadow of fear now, and he saw the woman, her hands squeezing flatly at the sides of her head, framing her agonized eyes and mouth; and in that still and terrible moment he knew that she must not be hurt, and also that to harm the man in front of him would be to mutilate himself in some obliquely bitter way.

He stumbled back, lowering the knife and turning his eyes once again to the figure that loomed in front of him. 'No — '

The huge fist struck his face again, a shattering blow that had terror behind it, and he fell, striking the wall before slumping heavily to the floor, his fading mind mercifully blanketing the pain as the knife slid searchingly between his ribs and the final darkness overtook him.

'Get up,' the big man said, panting. 'Get up, you dirty little toad.'

Then he saw the slowly spreading blood that came from beneath the motionless figure on the floor, 'Oh, God,' he said in a suddenly weak voice.

The woman said, 'What is it?' She moved shakily into the doorway, her hands still pressed against her face. She looked down and recoiled. 'Oh, *no!*' She spun away and leaned shudderingly against the door frame.

The man knelt and gingerly touched the body, fumbling at the wrist of a limply-sprawled arm. After a few moments he rose.

'I think he's dead,' he said thickly.

The woman moaned wretchedly. The man caressed his knuckles, scowling furiously, then abruptly dropped his hands to his sides. 'We've got to get out of here,' he said.

Bowed, the woman continued to sob. The man went rapidly to her and gripped her arm. 'Betty, for God's *sake*! We must *go*!'

The woman turned to him, her face haggard. 'But we can't just leave him here — '

'We have to,' the man said urgently. He stared at her uncomprehending face, then shook her again. 'What the hell else can we do? Do you mean we have to take him somewhere and dump him? How do we know they won't trace him back here somehow? We have to leave him and let somebody else find him, hope they think there were two of them, or something — ' His voice trailed away at the shocked expression on her face.

'You mean let Peter and me find him when we come down here again?' the woman said. 'Do you think I shall ever be able to come here again? Oh God, do you think I could *bear* to come, knowing what we'd find?'

She wrenched herself away from him.

'You don't realize what you've done,' she whispered. Her voice was barely audible.

'Done?' the man said. His voice rose. 'You bloody fool, I saved you from getting knifed, didn't I?'

The woman moved away from him into the living room. He followed her, his voice still high and furious. 'Well, didn't I?'

She turned towards him, her face an empty, tear-stained mask.

'Peter will never forgive me,' she said, 'when he finds out about us and my bringing you here.' Her voice was low and cold. 'Here, of all places.'

They stared at one another in a confusion of fear and sudden hatred as the light faded, and the shadows slowly filled the room and the still and silent kitchen beyond.

The Great Golf Mystery

The 4th Tee Murderer was a small man with rimless glasses, a mouse-like moustache, and a nervous twitch of the left nostril. This last acquisition was the only outward sign of emotion he had displayed since his trial, an understandably tension-fraught affair at which he had reluctantly been found guilty by twelve low-handicap men; and a concerted murmur of sympathy and admiration had sounded throughout the barred corridors of the prison on the morning he was taken to the death cell.

His lawyer visited him later that day, a trace of understandable embarrassment detectable in his demeanour. A previous commitment to participate in the local pro-am tournament had necessitated his delegating the case to a new — and, it now appeared, incompetent — substitute; and while his absence had been excusable, he felt that common courtesy demanded he put in an appearance, if only to say goodbye.

He was himself still a young man, but a nasty slice and a great deal of time spent in bunkers had matured him beyond his years, and his heart went out to the bowed figure he found listlessly toying with a putter, a pile of treasured score cards beside him.

The lawyer murmured a greeting, and seated himself.

The 4th Tee Murderer glanced up from his reverie, blinked, and twitched his left nostril at him.

'Ah, my dear fellow,' he said. His voice was low, but a hint of his old defiance could be heard beneath the dispirited tones. 'Good of you to come and see me off like this. Hope I haven't put you out in any way.'

'No, no,' the lawyer said, greatly relieved. His client's lack of animosity plainly labelled him a man of superior intellect and deep understanding, one who fully appreciated that you couldn't win them all. The lawyer's nervousness vanished, and his features assumed a look of sombre commiseration.

It was true that he had been booked to play in a foursome that afternoon, but he felt that, all things considered, it would have been churlish to mention it.

'My only wish is that I could do more. At times such as these, one experiences a sense of inadequacy comparable only to one's earliest youth, when the hook, slice, and top were one's shameful everyday companions.' He coughed delicately. 'Are you quite sure there is nothing that I can do? A fresh supply of practice balls? A new Swing-Rite Practice Companion with Double-Strength Air-Flite ball on Triple-Strength elastic, perhaps?'

The 4th Tee Murderer laughed bitterly.

'And what benefit would I derive from these things, these painful reminders of all that has made life worthwhile? They would only serve to make the end even more unendurable; though mind you, there might still be time to correct an unfortunate tendency to hook slightly with the dashed niblick.'

He paused thoughtfully, then sank back into his former state of despair. 'Ah, well. A flaw remains — perhaps symbolic of the unattainable perfection that we all seek and fail to find in this brief but blessed span, when we stride on springy turf — occasionally soggy, I grant you, especially in June, July, and August — learning to drive straight and true down the fairway of life, resisting the lure of bunker and the snare of rough, purifying ourselves little by little as we grope fumblingly towards par, and then — the Great Beyond.'

'Amen,' the lawyer said humbly.

The Murderer fixed him with a look of grim melancholy.

'Let me tell you the full bitter story,' he said. 'Let me tell you about the murder I committed on the fourth tee at Huggins' Hollow, the indubitably justifiable homicide that has resulted in my present incarceration and forthcoming demise. And I hope you have a strong stomach, for it is a tale that would sicken all but the stoutest. I speak metaphorically, you understand.' He paused courteously. 'If you can spare the time, of course. Sure I'm not keeping you from anything?'

'No, no,' the lawyer said. 'Not at all. I

shall be most interested. As a matter of fact, what with one thing and another, the details of the case — ' He coughed, eyed the bright sunlight that showed beyond the barred window, and suppressed a small inward sigh. 'Pray proceed.'

'It began,' the Murderer said heavily, 'as many other mornings have begun. I rose, showered, shaved, dressed, and proceeded downstairs to breakfast alone, leaving my wife to her slumber, or so I thought. And there I was, studying the previous day's match scores in the *Daily Golfer*, about to sip my fourth cup of tea, when it happened. There was a bellow in my ear of '*Surprise!*' — and I chokingly emerged from my cup to find my wife beside me, fully attired in — golfing clothes!'

The Murderer was pale, and his hands tautened on the shaft of the putter that he held; employing, the lawyer noted absently but approvingly, an orthodox reverse over-lapping grip.

'You will understand my dismay when I tell you that in our fifteen years of married life she had flatly refused to exhibit the faintest glimmer of interest in the finer things; contenting herself merely with running the house, painting impressionist landscapes which she sold for disgustingly large sums of money, writing bestselling novels and the occasional smash-hit musical, composing a symphony now and then, managing her dress salon, and so on. A wasted life,' the Murderer said sadly.

'However, it had happened at last. In her insatiable search for the new, the untried, she had finally decided to inflict herself on the most testing field of endeavour yet devised by man, confident in her butterfly fashion that she would sail blithely round in par as soon as she was let loose upon the hallowed ground.

'I pleaded, arguing the necessity for lessons, the need to parade one's naked unfitness before the humbling eye of the pro; but she would have none of it. She sulked, she whined. She said that I had ulterior motives in wishing her not to play. She said that I didn't love her. She said that she would go home to her mother.'

The Murderer sighed. 'You may wonder at this point why I failed to settle for what would unarguably have been the lesser of two evils; the sad truth being that, despite her inherently shallow nature and lack of imagination and initiative, I loved my wife. And despite my certain foreknowledge of the dark happenings ahead, I clung desperately to a vain hope that she would fall prey to some disease, preferably non-contagious, en route to the club; or fall and break an arm or leg before it became possible for her to shame me with her first attempted swing.

'Alas, it was not to be. At length I capitulated, and it was with a leaden heart that I watched her, one hour later, grasp my driver in a vice-like grip and address her ball for the very first time.

'The stance that she had chosen, despite repeated appeals on my own part, would be difficult to sum up in a phrase. Her toes were turned inward, her knees bent outward, her arms stiffly crooked at the elbow, and her posterior was as kickably projected as any man less iron-willed than myself could have wished. The total effect was similar to a clumsily-stuffed penguin I had once seen as a child, an item that had afforded me considerable amusement at the time, but now only caused me to reflect deeply on the tasteless humour of adolescence.

'She lifted her head towards the hole, presumably to verify that it had not been moved while she adopted her position, then swung the club — a sudden violent movement that was obviously intended to catch the ball while its thoughts were elsewhere.

'There was a muffled *click*, a square foot of turf sailed past my left ear, and I was astounded to see the ball limp to a halt over a hundred yards away, positioned directly in the centre of the fairway.

'I made haste to congratulate her on her success. To strike a golf ball at one's very first attempt is a quite remarkable achievement in itself, and its presence on the fairway, instead of somewhere to the extreme left or right of the tee, mercifully meant that we could immediately put distance between ourselves and the clubhouse, where horrified gazes were plainly visible at the window.

'I played my drive, a somewhat hurried affair that found its way into some long stuff over to the right, and we then proceeded to where my wife's ball lay.

'Halting beside it, and casting a cursory glance towards the distant flag, she stated that, as she now had the general feel of things, if I would be so good as to pass her one of the shorter clubs which looked to be a little more her size, she would proceed to knock the ball down the hole from where we stood.

'In vain I pointed out the sheer physical impossibility of her covering a distance of two hundred yards with a seven-, eight-, or nine-iron, but she brushed aside my pleas, impatiently snatched the eight from the bag, and once again addressed her ball.

'Here,' the Murderer said, following a slight pause during which he aged visibly (his hair turned almost white), 'we come to the point in the affair at which I felt the first teetering of my reason. As she swung — a clumsy, ill-coordinated affair that made her initial stroke look like a bit of business by Pavlova on one of her better nights — her left foot skidded inward on the turf, the club struck the ball, and simultaneously she pitched in the direction of the hole, regaining her balance only at the very last possible moment.

'With the full weight of her body behind the stroke the ball lifted, travelled in a graceful arc, the apex of which was approximately six feet from the ground, landed just short of the green, rolled twenty feet in a geometrically faultless straight line — and vanished into the hole.'

'Blessed indeed are the doings of the Lord,' the lawyer said emotionally. He was a churchgoing man and knew the value of prayer, teaching one as it did to keep one's head down. 'She was shown the Way.'

'Blessed my bloodshot eyeball,' the Murderer said bitterly. 'Dashed fishy, if you ask me. There was this woman, who'd never handled a club before in her dashed life, holing out with a double eagle on a hole that I've never been able to do in less than par, and using the wrong club to boot.'

He gnashed his teeth for a moment. 'Dashed fishy. It was almost as though — oh, well, never mind. When I recovered from the shock, I congratulated her again. I told her that by the greatest good luck, and assisted by a series of coincidences that made evolution look like mere child's play in comparison, she had just broken the club record for the first hole.

'Her reply, voiced petulantly, was that she had been perfectly confident of the outcome of her shot; and that she was disappointed only in the fact that it exposed my attempts to dissuade her from employing the club she had used as merely a clumsy attempt to ruin her game.'

The lawyer tutted disapprovingly.

'Tut you may,' the Murderer said, 'as would any civilized man. Stunned to silence, I holed out with a miserable six, and numbly followed her to the second tee.

'You know the hole, of course — a short affair liberally dotted with bunkers of the most vicious kind, and completed by a cunningly-positioned tree a little to the left of the tee. I watched in stricken silence as she again wrenched her limbs into the macabre pose that I had witnessed on the first tee, paused only to observe that the buttercups appeared to be a trifle early this year, then swiped at the ball.

'You could call it a slosh, if you prefer, or even a bash; but in no way could you label that fearsome wielding of the club a correct golfing stroke. The ball vanished, and it was only by craning my neck that I found it again, a diminishing speck that moved upward in an almost vertical line, curved sharply, then descended at frightful velocity to vanish into the topmost foliage of the tree. There was a sharp report, a shower of leaves, and the ball reappeared bouncing lightly onto the green, where it stopped three inches short of the hole.'

'Merciful Heaven!' the lawyer exclaimed. His face was pale.

'Merciful my ingrowing toenail,' the Murderer said querulously. 'If Heaven is so dashed merciful, what's it up to when it allows such incredible luck to fall on someone who has always laughed at the mere mention of the game, and whose demeanour indicated that she still considered it no great shakes and somewhat easier than falling off a log? Merciful Heaven, indeed,' the Murderer said, chafing visibly.

'Anyway, to cut down on the painful details, I hooked my tee shot, took five to get out of a bunker, and finished up with an eight for a triple bogey.'

The lawyer made incredulous noises.

'Quite so,' the Murderer said. 'We proceeded to the third tee, the four-hundred-yarder; where, my rapidly-failing grip on a sense of reality assured me, it would be quite impossible for her to achieve a distance of more than a hundred yards or so — particularly in view of the fact that she had insisted on retaining the eight-iron: a club, she said, that seemed to suit her style of play.

'The chances of her duplicating the incredible shot she had performed on the first hole were so minute as to be laughable; and yet it was with jangling nerves that I watched her as she squared up to the ball, paused only to comment that the daisies, too, appeared to be coming along nicely, and swung down on it.

'The result of this stroke,' the Murderer continued, his eyes glazed at the memory, 'can only be described as staggering, astounding, incredible, unbelievable, impossible, inconceivable, unheard-of, and beyond the bounds of reason. The ball took off, rose to a distance of eighteen inches above ground level, and maintained this height for approximately two hundred and seventy-five yards. It fell at last and rolled an additional fifty before coming to rest, perfectly positioned on a slight incline that bisects the fairway at that point.

'It was a full minute before I could gather my rapidly-disintegrating wits sufficiently to play my own shot. My drive, incredibly under the circumstances, was a moderately good one; and it was only after I had played my second shot and we had proceeded some distance down the fairway that I detected something distinctly odd about my wife's ball. We eventually reached it, and one glance was sufficient to explain its fantastic performance.

'The bottom edge of the club had sliced cleanly into the cover, almost removing it, but failing to sever the final three-quarters of an inch. The ball had then, of course, as any simpleton familiar with ffoulkes-ffarrington's Law could tell you, simply done a quarter backspin, followed by a quarter sidespin, opened out, and glided to the spot where it finished up.

'Wonderful thing, aerodynamics,' the Murderer said thoughtfully. 'Did you know that half a banana, sliced vertically, will fly from Dublin to New York if ejected from a small-bore cannon at a speed of one hundred and ninety-three point nought-nought-nought-seven miles per hour? Allowing for reasonable winds, of course. Nothing too blowy.

'Anyway, there it confronted us: the pitiable remains of what minutes before had been an excellent golf ball; quite unplayable now, of course. I explained to my wife that she was entitled to a replacement and, following her somewhat reluctant agreement, removed the corpse and placed a new ball where it had rested.

'She eyed it in a suspicious sort of way, rather as one might view a cigar that one has strong reason to suspect is loaded; but eventually she aimed her club and played her second shot.

'Again her left foot skidded inward, again she toppled in the direction of the hole, this time landing heavily on her side; at which point there was a sickening yet somehow heartwarming crack. I choked back my eager inquiry and watched the ball.

'Once again, unbelievably, it rose to a height of eighteen inches, sped towards the green, glanced off the lip of an intervening bunker, rose gracefully into the air, then sank out of sight, shortly reappearing as it rolled to a gentle halt a mere inch from the hole.

'On turning my blurred and unbeliev-ing gaze to my wife, to ascertain whether it was her neck, arm, leg, or simply her wrist that had been fractured, I was staggered to find her once again on her feet, angrily dusting herself down, the jagged remains of the club in her non-dusting hand.'

The lawyer made sounds of distress.

'You said it,' the Murderer said. 'A club with which I had chipped my way out of many a tight corner; especially at the club dances when that confounded Mrs. Huntington-Hereford got me lined up in her sights. She couldn't resist small men. Compact, she called me. Sturdy, too, as I recall. However . . . ' The Murderer dashed away a tear — whether for the demise of his number-eight iron, or the memory of missed opportunities at the club dances, the lawyer couldn't be sure.

'My wife brutally brandished the remains at me, loudly decrying the manufacturer who had supplied what she described as a flimsy excuse for a golfing stick. I was too heartbroken to reply, too ravaged by a bitter and lasting grief to do anything other than dumbly take the body from her careless grasp. I completed the hole with a further — ' The Murderer winced as he forced the hateful figures between clenched teeth. ' — seven strokes, but I was beyond caring by this time, chipping clumsily, putting like a lost soul.

'I was like a man in the grip of a nightmare as I followed her to the fourth and fatal tee. There, the fairway coiled before us, a fiendishly ingenious piece of golfing architecture, the sight of which has never failed to shatter the confidence of all but the half-witted and the short-sighted. Bunkers to the left, trees to the right, and a yawning chasm bisecting the fairway; the lip of its farther slope a full two hundred and five yards, two feet, nine and seven thirty-seconds of an inch away.

'Many golfers, as you know, have retreated gibbering from that spot, incurably afflicted with the Fourth Tee Twitch: that dreaded malady which renders the imbibing of liquid impossible other than through a straw, and induces in the victim a compulsion to buy and store unreasonably vast quantities of golf balls. My wife merely cast a nonchalant glance at this bleakly intimidating terrain, made a comment to the effect that it was about time that it was tidied up a bit, and contorted herself into her customary striking stance.

'Until this point her performance, fantastic though it had undoubtedly been, was not entirely beyond the bounds of reason. Her use of the club, while in itself undeniably horrifying to the sensitive observer, had resulted in nothing more than a remarkable series of freak shots: all physically possible, if not exactly probable in such unprecedented profusion.

'She had also, of course, been more than fortunate in that certain static objects arranged for the purpose of creating hazards to impede the player had instead perversely aided her to achieve the incredible results I had witnessed on that grim and godless morning. It is true that the odds against such a sequence of improbabilities are zillions to one against — ninety-eight zillion or thereabouts, I make it — but they are, at least, minimally possible.

'However, at this stage in the proceedings it was at last made abundantly clear that all logic had deserted this earthly realm, and that chaos, cold and uncaring, now reigned in its stead.

'The raven,' the Murderer said, with an abrupt change of gear that had the lawyer floundering for a moment or two, 'is traditionally a symbol of evil; a line of thought to which I now subscribe with the utmost vigour, for I was about to witness a demonstration that bracketed it once and for all with those things that are so obviously thrust upon us by the boys downstairs. Things like the fourteenth hole at Snidgely Common,' he finished broodingly.

'Anyway, she swung at the ball, an action that was accompanied by the tuneful and unmistakable snap of a disintegrating garter. With an exclamation of annoyance she cast the club from her and commenced to rummage beneath her skirt; while I, with faith suddenly reignited in my bosom, watched her ball rise at a limp tangent, fall to the ground a mere ten yards from where we stood, then trickle from sight into the yawning mouth of the ravine.

'And then it happened. A sinister flapping sound commenced, and before my eyes the black and malevolent figure of a raven rose from the murky depths. Clenched tightly in its claws was my wife's ball. It turned a beadily thoughtful eye in my direction, sneered visibly, then turned and flew away from where we stood, headed directly down the centre of the fairway. Several yards short of the distant green it relinquished its grip on my wife's ball, which fell on level turf, bounded a short distance, and became stationary approximately six inches from the hole.'

A deathly hush filled the small, drab room, a silence that was broken at last by the lawyer's tremulous tones.

'At such times there is little one can say.'

'Permit me to differ,' the Murderer grated. 'At such times there is a good deal one can say, and I count myself fortunate that my vocabulary is at least adequately equipped for such an occasion. As the power of speech returned, I utilized it to the full. I spoke. I employed the sum total of the invective at my command, unleashing on the elements a tirade that would not have disgraced a regimental sergeant-major whose foot has just been run over by a fifty-ton tank.'

The lawyer smiled reminiscently. 'Your story puts me in mind of my own reaction to recent trying circumstances. A muffed putt on the seventh only last Wednesday — '

The Murderer shook his head warningly. 'To continue. As I paused to gather breath to continue my harangue, she intervened. She said she had no idea what I was talking about, that if I wished to employ disgusting language I could do so elsewhere, that I was nothing more than a rotten sport, insanely jealous of her obvious talent for a game at which I appeared to be somewhat less than competent, and that she was going home to her mother. And then,' the Murderer said, his voice a low, sudden sob, 'she said — It.'

The lawyer winced, and summoned an inadequate tut.

'She said,' the Murderer said, his voice that of a man who has heard the Devil's testament, 'that it was, after all, simply a footling game, a pastime for retired bank managers and the feeble-minded. What person in his right senses, she wished to know, could actually derive enjoyment from striking a small ball with a stick that has a knob on the end, and frequently subjected to the buffering of the elements in the process? Who, she jeeringly queried, but an adolescent numbskull would thrill to the prospect of pursuing that same small ball for a distance of several miles, weaving from rough to hedge to bunker to ditch, exhausting both body and patience in the process, and building up a bigger crop of ulcers than you could shake a stick at?

'There was more, much more, but it became simply a blur of words, a foully blasphemous sound that had to be stopped at all costs. And while red mist roiled before my eyes, it was done. I used my wedge,' the Murderer said. His eyes were moist with tears. 'A crisp, wristy hit, with plenty of follow-through. She felt no pain, I am sure.'

His head sank on his chest, and he was silent at last.

'You were sorely tried,' the lawyer said hoarsely. He felt deeply for this man. 'Under such brutally provocative circumstances, how can I say what I myself, despite the appalling prospect of having to conduct my own defence on such a charge, might have done? A rather intriguing example of this particular predicament,' the lawyer said, his voice adopting a professional drone, 'was the case of Crown vs. Gubbins — '

'What have I done?' the Murderer cried. The lawyer blundered to a halt, losing the thread of things. 'What have I done, what have I done?'

The lawyer endeavoured to soothe him. 'A perfectly understand — '

'But she was right!' the Murderer cried. He leaped to his feet, wild-eyed, and cast his putter from him with a gesture of sudden loathing. 'What is it but a recreation for the shallow and childish, an obsessive drug that blinds us to the true values? The human relationship, the bond between man and man, and — ' He sobbed. ' — man and his mate — *there* you have the true reason for existence!'

'What?' the lawyer cried, aghast.

The Murderer dispersed the pile of treasured score cards with a well-aimed kick. 'I have been blind, blind! Why, when it is too late, has the truth made itself known to me? She was right! It *is* simply a footling game, a pastime for retired bank managers and the feeble-minded. What person in his right senses *would* actually derive enjoyment from striking a small ball with a stick that has a knob on the end, and frequently subjected to the buffeting of the elements in the process? Who but an adolescent numbskull — ?'

He spoke on, but in the lawyer's ears it became simply a blur of words, a foully blasphemous sound that had to be stopped at all costs.

And while red mist roiled before his eyes, the lawyer reached blindly for the Murderer's discarded putter . . .

★   ★   ★

'Ghastly business, ghastly,' the warden said. He coughed, distinctly ill-at-ease. 'No, I mean, really. Er — rather unusual, too, I should have thought. Surely something with a little more loft to it — ? Oh well, no matter. What I fail to understand — ah — what has me totally baffled — er, that is to say, in a nutshell, if you follow me: why did you — ah — do it?'

The lawyer sat before the warden in his office, his eyes downcast, his face wan. A guard stood at his shoulder, the murder weapon in his hand.

The lawyer opened his mouth, closed it, opened it again, croaked, then was silent.

The warden cracked his knuckles nervously.

'Company cramping your style, possibly? Quite understandable. Embarrassed and so forth. Man in your position — ah — Jenkins.' The guard stiffened to attention. 'Might be better if you waited outside. You can leave the — ah — thing.' The guard exited.

'Well, now,' the warden said, leaning forward and shuffling his feet beneath the desk. 'Better, eh? Free to talk, and all that.' He fiddled with the putter. 'Jolly nice little club, this. Very much the style of thing I was using myself a year or so back. Rather too much meat on the shaft, I found — however . . . ' He pushed it away. 'You were saying?'

The lawyer opened his mouth again, croaked tentatively, then spoke in low, broken tones.

'He insisted on describing in detail the events that had resulted in his incarceration and forthcoming demise, warning me at the time that a strong stomach would be an advantage, as it was a tale that would sicken all but the stoutest. He spoke metaphorically, he assured me. It began, it seems, as many other mornings had begun . . . '

The warden settled back in his chair, adopting an expression of polite interest. He had, if truth be told, been booked to play in a foursome later that afternoon; but he felt that, all things considered, it would have been churlish to mention it . . .

Mirror, Mirror

Kevin Sharp was twenty-seven when he fulfilled the fairly commonplace, and generally calculating, ambition of many by marrying the boss's daughter.

Despite the manifest advantages of such an alliance, this particular coupling was in fact precipitated by an element not all that often found in marriage, and almost unheard-of in one so ostensibly expedient. Simply, this deviation from the norm consisted of a remarkably high degree of instant rapport between them, a promise of rare compatibility that was mutually detected at the moment of introduction. They were in tune at once, counterpointing each other with the effortless smoothness of a well-rehearsed musical duo; his laconic, slightly wry humour matched by hers. Apart from her more obvious attractions she was, Kevin was delighted to find, the first woman he had met capable of producing remarks which he would have been quite happy to have had credited to himself.

Physically, too, they were beautifully-paired. She was fair: near-blonde, slender, and four inches shorter than his raven-haired five feet eleven inches. Standing in a corner of the main studio, ignoring the innocuous drone of office party talk around them, but always conscious of her father's benevolently cautious eye aimed in their direction from the other side of the room, Kevin traded admiring stares and lightly bantering conversation with Moira Langley, and amusedly wondered if falling in love could really be as painlessly simple as this.

Apparently it could. A fortnight after meeting they slept together: a relaxing, soothing liaison where they meshed, like two meticulously-engineered components of the same machine. The following day they became engaged; two months later they were married,

Kevin had joined Langley, Labone & Partners as studio manager. They returned from their honeymoon to find George Langley sufficiently reconciled to the situation to elevate him to the level of a junior partnership, a step-up that was accompanied by the hint of even greater advancement in the future. Within eighteen months the company's masthead had been amended to Langley, Labone, Sharp & Partners, a development that Kevin and Moira celebrated with a month in the Bahamas, pleasurably anticipating the further jaundiced scrutiny of their less solidly-based contemporaries.

They were, understandably, the envy of their friends. Despite the fact that she was the boss's daughter, their evenly floating relationship was so plainly genuine, so patently unforced, that it automatically became the focal point for the collective wistful glances of those whose own marriages existed — or had already foundered — on rather more traditionally rocky terrain. Kevin and Moira knew it, were entertained by it, and mutually delighted in the lack of effort required to maintain this equilibrium.

They had been married for a little over three years when it suddenly dawned on Kevin that he was becoming unutterably bored by their relationship.

Dismayed and painful consideration soon told him why. Living with Moira was like living with his own reflection; endless posturing in front of a mirror that distorted the surface details of its resultant image while simultaneously preserving the true nature of its source. Predictable, Kevin thought dully; that was the word. It was as though his shadow danced in constant attendance, arriving at the same whim, the same conclusion, the same decision at exactly the same point in time. It was, in fact, a genuinely uncanny alliance that had been doomed to failure precisely because of their enviously-observed similarities; a narcissistic, bruiseless existence that now appalled him with its promise of well-oiled infinity.

He could have tried arguing with her, employing deliberate provocation, but he shrank from that. Apart from the fact that it would be a kind of self-flagellation, there was always his position in the firm to be considered. He was a fully-fledged partner, but there was never any question that George Langley held the reins firmly in both hands, and was perfectly capable of employing them in his direction should he have reason to suspect that he was in any way giving Moira a hard time.

The company was opening a branch in Los Angeles shortly after this stunning realisation hit him. To his relief, George Langley asked him to direct the operation during its initial stages, a task that was likely to keep him occupied for several months at least.

He and Moira had just purchased a new house in Bridgeport, but hadn't yet given a great deal of thought to the question of decorations and additional furniture. He persuaded her to stay behind and handle these herself, coupled with the promise that he would make it back each weekend.

It was a sensible arrangement, with no hint of anything other than a genuine desire to see that their new home was completed as soon as possible. It might even help in the long term, he told himself. Maybe the break will have a recuperative effect; absence makes the heart grow fonder, that kind of thing. The thought had an insubstantial feel to it, its hollow fragility mocking him as he kissed her goodbye and boarded the plane.

An hour after arriving in Los Angeles, he met Lynne Craddock.

She had been hired by Langley during one of his preliminary scouting expeditions of the new territory, and he hadn't known what to expect. Langley had described her as an ideal secretary for use at executive level. Kevin found a dark, faintly Spanish woman, with an apparently disciplined smouldering quality that he immediately found rather irritating. She was attractive, and her file of employment told him that she was a year older than him. Bitter, explosive type, Kevin decided sourly; and wondered why Langley had hired her instead of some cool, detached woman who would surely have been more suitable.

Maybe he had a secret taste for that kind of prickly exotica. Kevin shrugged, and got on with the multi-detailed business of organisation.

He found that working with her only increased his irritation. She seemed efficient, but she emanated an air of resentment in his presence, as though he were guilty of some undetectable — to him, at least — social failing that her own good manners forbade her from pointing out. Kevin bit back the sarcasm that he found regularly on the tip of his tongue, and maintained a curt impartiality that seemed the best way of handling such additional burdens to his already overloaded plate.

Late on the Friday, they were the last two in the office. They were checking estimates for equipment, another aggravating chore that should have been completed earlier in the week. Her excuses had been reasonable, but he had a plane to catch in little over an hour and was both exasperated and tired.

'Hell,' he said. He threw his stylus on the desk, from where it bounced out of sight to the floor. They had just compared figures for the third time, once more finding them differing by several hundred seemingly unaccountable dollars. He glared at the sprawl of papers in front of him, hating their impassive refusal to give up their secrets. 'Look, this is getting just

169

plain ridiculous, and I have to get to the airport. I'm going to have to ask you to work on these over the weekend and get them tied up by Monday morning.'

He sensed her stiffen.

He said, carefully, 'I don't like asking you to do this, you understand, but when all's said and done, they are your responsibility. If you'd only raised it in the middle of the week when we had — '

'You know as well as I do that it hasn't been possible to get to them before this,' Lynne Craddock said, angrily. The smouldering quality was very near the surface now, could almost literally be felt. Kevin found himself loathing her with a tight-jawed, sinewy intensity. 'And you damned well know the hours I've had to work to get things this far. In any case, why should it be *my* figures that are wrong? I know my own mathematical ability, but I certainly don't know yours.'

She reached out a hand to pick up the sheet that held his own calculations. Furious, Kevin grabbed at her wrist.

It was like an explosion, the slamming together of two ingredients that remained only potentially dangerous as long as they were kept from direct physical contact with each other. He found that their eyes were locked, and that he was shaking, almost palsied.

'God,' he said, thickly. He stood and pulled her around the desk to him, feeling her reciprocal clawing the moment she was against him.

It was a ferocious, bruising encounter, one that was later continued at her apartment where he spent the night. There was none of the placidly pleasant, almost mathematically balanced, activity that habitually took place between himself and Moira. This was urgent, hungry business, unlike anything that he had known before, and seemingly insatiable.

The following morning he managed to get a cancelled booking on the New York flight. He left Lynne crying in a taxi outside the airport — a still-rational precautionary corner of his mind told him that such a place, even in a relatively strange city, was not an ideal site at which to be seen with an attractive and obviously distressed woman — and it was only when he and his fellow-passengers were somewhere over Kansas that the full implications of the situation hit him like a blow from a fist composed of solid ice.

He was married to the boss's daughter, and now he had become inextricably involved with a member of the staff: a passionate, soul-wrenching relationship that he already knew would flatly refuse to be denied. During the past fourteen hours he had discovered depths of longing inside himself that he had never dreamed were there, coupled with an ability to stir emotions that was like a blinding revelation.

It was a hopeless situation. The ways open to them were grimly apparent, none of them offering an even half-satisfactory answer. He could, presumably, set up house with Lynne, sustaining the empty mockery that his marriage had become by sticking painfully to the already-promised routine of returning home at the week-ends, but it would be risky. And what about when the branch was established and he was required to return to New York to resume his duties there? She could give up her job and follow him, he supposed — he never doubted for a moment that she would be willing to follow such a course of action — but apart from the fact that it might possibly arouse suspicions among the L.A. staff, it just wouldn't work.

He wanted her permanently, as his wife. He knew this with unswerving certainty, as surely as he knew that the sun rose daily in the east. He wanted to live with her, to watch the endless unfolding of points of contrast with himself, to share the daily miracle of being with her, his blood and imagination stirred by her presence. He thought, painfully, about his marriage; the dream that had only been a dream, now sliding smoothly down to drown in its own interminably boring lack of conflict.

There was divorce, of course. He thought about what this would mean, both from the business and social points of view. It would be death, on both counts. No outsider, seeing the sleek surface of his marriage, would accept that he was doing anything other than discarding the perfect, loyal partner to satisfy some lunatic passion, the act of an inherently unstable personality who would logically be a bad bet for really responsible employment.

Because he would have to look for a job, naturally. The moment divorce was mentioned, he'd be out on his ear, partner or no partner. And this might eventually destroy them.

He knew that it was possible for relationships to stay constant, and even blossom, in the face of such difficulties; but he was still enough of a pragmatist to seriously doubt that theirs would survive if subjected to too much in the way of deprivation. In itself it was a miracle, but it was an earthbound miracle, composed of heat and flesh and emotional collision. It required cushioning, conditions where it could rest and recuperate between the bouts of violence, both verbal and physical, that would surely be the endless stimulating pattern.

He was still warring with himself when the plane landed. Moira was there to meet him: cool, affectionate, pleased to see him in the way that one accepted a foregone

conclusion. She made only a passing reference to the call that he had somehow
remembered to make on the previous evening.
He winced as he recalled it, desperately
hoping that the guilt in his voice had been
neutralised by distance and a thankfully
indifferent line. As he kissed her smiling
mouth, he wondered what his own face
showed.

He struggled through what was left of
the weekend somehow. Moira was initially
talkative, producing fragments of fabric
and details of colour schemes that she
abandoned as soon as she sensed his
out-of-kilter mood. He pleaded overwork,
a reasonable explanation that she plainly
accepted, and which gave him the excuse
to spend much of the time ostensibly
dozing. He tried to hide his relief and
mounting excitement as he kissed her
goodbye and boarded the plane on the
Monday morning.

He saw as little of Lynne as possible
— during office hours. But as soon as
they were finished, even before they left
the building, it resumed, ravenous and
compelling. His last reluctant hope for a

return to unruffled normality vanished, and he knew that this was final, a binding contract that only an accident or death could destroy.

A routine was established, an uneasy, fretful compromise that he temporarily accepted. During office hours their initial reaction to each other continued, something that in itself was not difficult to maintain. Every evening that contained no business appointment, he spent at her apartment.

These times of privacy only confirmed his belief in the permanency of their passion. He was alive at last, roused to a pitch of response and awareness that made his previous existence appear as a series of pale, detached shadows, insubstantially based on self-love and self-admiration. This was tangible by comparison: warm and solid, an environment from which he could look at the world and its wonders with freshly unblinkered eyes.

They talked about Moira often: Lynne with bitter resentment, and sometimes despair; Kevin with questing hopelessness. Despite the quality of their relationship, he was essentially a non-violent person, and the restrictions that this automatically placed on his search for a solution meant that he baulked utterly at the idea of murder. It was something that happened every day, something that a great many people got away with, but it was not for him. Oddly, he could imagine circumstances where he would kill Lynne, but not Moira. Moira was his mirror-image, essentially without passion in the way that he had come to understand it, but still a part of him. Lynne was an individual, emotional quick-silver, with the violence never far below the surface and readily capable of igniting his own previously low-key responses.

The weekend trips back to Moira were purgatory, but he preserved what seemed to be an acceptable façade, most of the time managing to simulate something resembling nonchalant affection. Moira seemed much the same as ever; light, gay, full of plans for the house. There were periods when an unaccustomed touch of timidity seemed to shadow her behaviour, but he found this an understandable reaction to his own occasional lapses into introspection. At such times he hated himself for what he was doing, but he was committed. The thought of Lynne clouded his mind and eyes so that he was virtually blind to his surroundings and the people in them, impatient only for the moment when he could be with her again.

He assumed on the evidence that Moira suspected nothing. He wondered what she would have done about it if she had hired a private investigator; he was sickened by the thought, picturing how such a course of action would inevitably distort its findings, reducing the relationship to something which could be made to look dirty and shameful if nothing but the cold facts were catalogued on paper.

It wasn't a possibility that he took very seriously, but at one point in his thinking he did take it to the extent of mentally putting himself in Moira's shoes. The answer was reassuring. If the reverse had been the case, if he'd had reason to suspect that Moira had established a similar relationship, the answer was that he would have done nothing about it. He would have waited, shaken, but confident that she would return after recognising her affair for what it must surely have been, a dalliance that could only temporarily ruffle the smooth surface of their marriage.

Poor Moira, he thought wryly, poor kid. If only she knew what had happened to him, the strength of the emotional upheaval that had turned him head-over-heels and which still had him spinning like some irrational perpetual motion machine.

Two-and-a-half months after their initial physical encounter, Lynne told him that she was pregnant.

He received the news with something very like calm acceptance. Although he and Moira had never produced children, something that neither of them had greatly cared about, the ultimate confirmation of his love for Lynne had been when he realised that this was an essential part of his feelings for her, the desire to father her child. If the will, he thought, was all too appropriately the parent to the deed, then this was another rock-solid certainty that all the precautions in the world would not have been able to prevent.

He also knew, regretfully, that he would have to kill Moira.

It was now the only way. If this conception had not taken place, it was at least on the cards that the present arrangement would have blundered fitfully along until the time of his permanent return to New York, when they might have worked something out. It had been a slim chance, but marginally possible.

But now his child was going to be born, a situation that changed everything. There could be no back-street upbringing, no fatherless infant whose mother was maintained by cheques from some shadowy benefactor. The alternatives offered by the adoption authorities and the abortionist never entered his mind. The child would grow up in a home with both a mother and father present, its own natural parents tending it through its vulnerable formative years.

He said nothing to Lynne about his decision, but he was sure she knew, and also that she didn't care. The primitive part of her make-up, always present, was

4magnified to a degree where only the protection of her child and her feelings for him mattered, an instinctive withdrawal to essentials that he sensed were prepared to ignore the rules of law and society.

And it must be now, he told himself, while the resolve is strong. If he waited, too much thinking about it could undermine his nerve. No, he mustn't hesitate. He and Lynne nodded a final goodbye to each other as he left for the airport that Friday afternoon, twin signals of decision that told him she understood and that she would be waiting for him.

He had only a casual interest in the daily quota of violence reported by the media, and crime fiction was something that he read only occasionally. He was, in a sense, completely unfitted for such a venture, but this in itself was a kind of advantage. His normal attitude to such things was known to his acquaintances, which meant that it was extremely unlikely that suspicion of any sort would be directed towards him on the social level.

There would be no reason why it should.

The timing would have all the external appearances of an accident, one of those day-to-day fatalities that struck with sudden, meaningless cruelty, with nothing but innocent grief to show for its passage.

There must, of course, be no hint that it could be anything other than this. If only the slightest untoward thing was noticed by some sharp-eyed observer, it could all too easily become a matter for police investigation, and he knew what that meant. In such instances, the husband immediately and quite understandably became the principal suspect, his private activities thoroughly investigated,

He must run no risk of any kind. However it was done, it would have to be uncomplicated; a safe, simple routine that required no careful memorising of a detailed plan or timetable. He remembered reading somewhere that cleverness of this kind often resulted in the cases that were the easiest to break down: the often brilliantly-conceived webs of apparent accident or suicide and unshakeable alibi, which ultimately trapped their creators in the strands of their own ingenuity.

He had no intention of being snared in this way. When he did it, it would be direct, uncomplicated and final. And it would succeed, because it had to, ensuring that the chain of subsequent events betrayed no detectable connection.

It was impossible for Lynne and himself to be married when their child was born, but the circumstances of her own birth and situation had already inspired his draft scenario as to how this would eventually come about. Her mother, unmarried and alone, had died when she was only months old, and she herself had moved to Los Angeles from Tampico shortly before being employed by Langley, so had no real local intimates. Even with this promising foundation on which to build, what happened after Moira's death would inevitably be more complex than the event itself. But, he told himself doggedly, it would work, handled with cunning and care. There would be Lynne's nervous breakdown; followed by her departure for several months to another part of the country, ostensibly to recuperate with helpful friends; the careful choosing of discreet foster-parents before the birth; her return to L.A.; their chance meeting at the office at the time of her social call on old colleagues, and his contrived visit there if one should be necessary; their publicly-displayed mutual commiseration on their respective misfortunes; and, at last, marriage and the adoption of a fictional unmarried sister's child, following her accidental death.

It would be tricky and it would take time, perhaps even a year or two, but it could be done, he was sure. Thank God, he thought, for their initial public clash of personalities. Despite the intensity of their passion, they had been discreet about their meetings, and he was more convinced than ever that if Moira had suspicions she would have kept them to herself, her vanity refusing to accept that the danger to their marriage was anything other than temporary.

So he had nothing to fear from that source. The only real danger visible at this point was from himself, if he should fall into the ever-waiting trap of attempted cleverness.

Direct, he thought again, uncomplicated, final.

He rang for a drink, and began to plan.

*　　*　　*

He took a cab from the airport and a train from the city. Moira no longer met him off the plane; the mutually-agreed reason for this being that she too had her hands full and that it really was rather too far to come when it was a comparatively simple business for him to make his own way home.

At Bridgeport he took another cab, cautiously relieved to note that the driver was one who had taken him home before and who clearly recognised him. He settled back against the cushions, studying the back of his head and considering what sort of witness he was likely to make if called on.

He was tense, but not overly so. The drinks that he'd had on the plane had taken the edge off his nervousness, and he was sure that, externally at least, the impression that he gave was one of

185

normality. It was possible that this might be important at this stage. In any investigation, this stranger's testimony could easily tip the balance, decide the police whether or not his behaviour immediately preceding the accident warranted further enquiries being made.

On an impulse, he said, 'What's the weather going to be doing over the weekend? Any idea?'

'Dry,' the driver replied. 'Light winds, I think they said.' He eased the cab around a corner with nonchalant expertise. 'Golf?'

Kevin laughed. 'I was thinking about it, but we've still got a lot to sort out in our new place. I'd sure like to get out and shake the rust off, though.'

For the remainder of the journey they discussed the current form of Tiger Woods; the driver critically, Kevin with concealed delight.

Minutes later, they stopped at the end of the freshly-asphalted road. As the cab drove off and Kevin walked up the path, he saw that there was a light visible through the front door, and another behind the drawn curtains of the living room. He took out his key, unlocked the door, and went in. As he was closing it, Moira's voice said, 'Kev?'

He turned, startled. It was not the fact of this almost instantaneous greeting in itself that had caught him by surprise, but the direction from which it appeared to have come. He raised his head, his heart running a shade faster, and stared at Moira where she stood at the top of the stairs.

When he had been making his plans, the location of the accident had suggested itself more or less automatically. It had to be indoors, concealed from possible witnesses; which meant that there was only one place in the house where it could happen without in any way appearing to have been contrived.

It had been his intention to go upstairs directly on entering the house; and once there, call her. The inference would have been that he had brought her a present of some kind, possibly something for utilization in the bedroom. He would have met her at the top of the stairs, manoeuvred her to face down them again, and then pushed.

He felt a chill pass over him, like the shadow of a cloud. There was no earthly reason why she should not have been upstairs at the time of his arrival, but now the situation seemed somehow unreal; a nightmare stage production where actors moved at the behest of some malignant director, acting out his darkly devised narrative. She stood looking down at him, her face shadowed; the poised victim, her position marked with scratches of invisible chalk.

He felt slightly sick. He placed his bag on the floor, and said, 'Hi. Don't come down. Something I want to show you.'

Smiling, he advanced up the stairs.

She waited for him without moving. She had one hand on the rail, the other down by her side — clenched stiffly, he now saw. It was almost as though she knew what was about to happen and was tensing herself for it, seeing his approach as the measured step of the executioner, relentless and inescapable.

That was impossible, but he sensed her

tautness as he stepped up to stand beside her on the landing. And still, inexplicably, she faced away from him down the stairs, a rigidly-posed partner in some insane ritual dance that demanded to be performed.

He stepped behind her, placed his hands flat against her shoulders, and pushed with all his strength.

She whimpered slightly as she toppled out and flailed jarringly down to the hallway. When she was almost there, he caught a glimpse of her face, an image that stayed clamped in his mind like the result of an imperfect camera shot: blurred, but sufficient in detail. Her expression showed shock, but something else, too; something that to Kevin looked strangely like remorse.

She hit the polished wooden floor, slid two or three feet, and lay still.

He steeled himself before going down to her. Reason had already told him that it was possible that he would find himself in the sickening position of having to administer a coup de grâce should the fall have actually failed to kill her. This would be risky, but perhaps necessary. He was breathing raggedly as he knelt beside her, but even before his damp fumbling failed to detect any pulse in her limp wrist, the position of her head told him that he had been spared the performance of this final brutality.

He picked her up and carried her into the living room, placing her carefully on the couch, and as he did so the barrier that had somehow neutralised any deep emotion that he might have felt before this dissolved abruptly.

He sat on a nearby chair, weeping. What was done was irrevocable, and it was only with the completion of the actual deed that he found himself capable of a return to something close to true rationality. For the first time in months, he caught a fleeting glimpse of the strange balance between them, as it had existed before his realisation and subsequent deceit: a unique thing of anticipation and echo, doomed by its own perfection. It had not been her fault, or his. It had simply been one of those unfeeling quirks of fate that seemingly at random select certain people, and then inexorably steer them towards its inescapable outcome, victims of some warped caprice whose only possible ending was tragedy.

It had been an important part of his plan that he phone the local hospital as soon as it was over. His story was simplicity itself: his arrival home, his announcement of his presence, the unseen fall down the stairs as he waited for her in the living room. That was all. Medical examination would confirm the time of her death, and surely that would be all that would be needed by investigating officials; no evidence of physical conflict, no sign of any kind that the real circumstance were in any way different from what he had told them. They would simply find a desolate man and his dead wife, the quality of whose relationship would be solemnly sworn by literally dozens of convincingly appalled acquaintances.

It slowly dawned on him that he had been sitting there a long time. He looked at his watch, and was shocked to find that almost thirty minutes had passed since last checking it before starting up the path to the house. But somehow this time-lag, that should have terrified him with the way that it introduced a suggestion of possible deceit into his story, failed to stir him in any great measure. Either they believed him, or they didn't. There was no incriminating evidence of any kind, and he found that he was now contemptuous of mere suspicion. He shrugged mentally, recognising his apathy as the inevitable reaction to the destruction of part of himself, repugnant to him though it had become; the smashing of the mirror, removing for all time the opportunity to study himself, to preen and to admire the image that he presented to the world.

He shook his head, rose, and went to the telephone. As he picked up the receiver, the front door chimes rang.

He stood poised uncertainly for a moment, then replaced the receiver. It was pointless to pretend that he hadn't heard, or that the house was empty. The lights were on in both the hallway and the living room, providing clear evidence of occupancy. No, hesitancy could only work against him. Far better to answer the door immediately, his bloodless complexion now facing him from the mirror above the telephone table giving veracity to his story — and especially to his newly-added coda, that he had collapsed on finding the body.

He went to the door, and opened it. A man stood on the step; a tall, heavy, blondish man, possibly a year or two his senior. He looked, oddly, to be extremely nervous. Kevin had never seen him before in his life.

The man said, 'Well? May I come in?' He seemed to take it for granted that this would be acceptable.

He walked heavily past Kevin, turned, and faced him. He looked drawn, but resolute. He said, thickly, 'I can see she's told you. It must have been a hell of a shock.'

Kevin said nothing, staring at him. The man said, 'Look, I can understand how you feel, but you must try and see our side of it, too. I never wanted to get into anything like this, and neither did Moira, but it's an honest-to-God fact that we couldn't help ourselves.' His mouth became stubborn. 'I don't think that very many people would understand, not really. It's a one-in-a-million thing that you just . . . '

He talked on, with muted, shame-faced passion.

Kevin watched him, silently. It was as though he was seeing the gradual reassembly of a mirror; a slow, agonised exercise that was now permitting him to view its other side, seeing at last beyond the bland surface image that it had always presented to him. Odd parts of this man's discourse were new — something about furniture design and manufacture, his own business — but these were details only. For the most part the pattern was painfully familiar, a logical reflection of events that must surely have concluded as they were doing, reaching the end of the only path that had ever been open to them.

Balance, he thought. The completion of the circle, pre-ordained and perfect in its simplicity. Me, Moira. Moira, me. He found with a calmly accepting absence of surprise that he was actually amused by the sheer structural beauty of it all, the immaculate precision of its resolution.

He said, 'I didn't know. I'm sorry.' The man's floundering tumble of words trickled to a halt. He stared, uncomprehendingly, his mouth slightly open. Kevin felt a surge of something darkly bitter at the back of his throat, a grotesque and barely containable desire to laugh. He shook his head. 'If I had, there'd have been no need — '

He stopped, indifferent to his indiscretion but choked into silence by the relentlessly growing pressure inside him.

After a moment, the man said, slowly, 'What are you talking about? You mean she didn't tell you?' His eyes slid past Kevin, focussing on something beyond the open living room door. He stiffened abruptly, his face shocked with sudden disbelief.

He made an anguished sound, and lurched forward. Seconds later, his sobs could be heard, muffled against the sprawled, waxen figure that he pawed with large, hopeless hands.

Watching him, in a distant way sharing his grief, Kevin thought briefly and with deep sadness of Lynne and the unborn child that he would now never see, feeling them drift away from him into a future where he knew he had no part, leaving behind an emptiness in which the dream had died in unison with Moira.

For every action, he thought, tiredly — how did it go? — there is an equal and opposite reaction. Something like that. And never, never more reasonably than now. Again, he marvelled at the completeness and absolute symmetry of the pattern, the clinical rightness of its logic.

Direct, he told himself, uncomplicated, final.

His laughter welled, a suddenly unstoppable flood. He stood there, head thrown back, the harshly raucous sound filling the house as he waited for the weeping man's return.

Dark Destiny

Her mother was talking on the hallway phone when she left the house, automatically restricting their goodbyes to a mutual waving of hands. She closed the door behind her and began to walk down the garden path, only then becoming aware of the man stood motionless on the opposite pavement, staring fixedly in her direction.

Even though he was at least thirty yards away she registered a clear image of unblinking eyes, sunk deep in an unhealthily pale face and now rigidly focussed on her and her movements. Discomfited, she quickly averted her own gaze, glancing up and down the street. Other people had just passed the house, near-neighbours that she often chatted with at the bus stop. Relieved by their proximity and still keeping her eyes averted, she reached the pavement and headed briskly away from him towards the main road.

Odd, she thought. Pretty creepy, really, although not enough to rouse real alarm; not in broad daylight and with other people nearby. There'd been nothing threatening about his pose, anyway; simply the suggestion of a protracted vigil, as though he'd been standing there for a while, waiting for her to emerge.

The raincoat he was wearing was unseasonable, but its seemingly inappropriate usage could have been linked to the matter of his health, she reflected. Perhaps he was someone she'd encountered at the hospital, his bad colour evidence of an ongoing condition; some mildly unstable ex-patient who'd developed a fixation on her while he'd been in her care. Without being overtly vain she knew she was attractive, and that kind of thing had happened before; but if this was another case of it, she hadn't recognised him. People looked different in street clothes, though, she reminded herself; so it was perfectly possible that he'd passed through her hands at some forgotten point, subsequently fantasising —

She heard footsteps behind her, rapidly

approaching. Then he was beside her. 'Excuse me.' His breathing was wheezily laboured. 'I'm sorry to trouble you, but I wonder if you could help me.'

Despite the disquiet she'd experienced at the time of her first sighting of him, the fact that he appeared to be ailing in some way had tempered her unease with a modicum of sympathy. Now, reluctantly dragging her eyes away from the retreating backs of the street's other inhabitants, she turned her head in his direction, and what she saw reinforced this aspect of her initial reaction.

His paleness contained a greyish shadow, and his eyes were dark-ringed with the fatigue of illness. He was around fifty or so, she judged, although he could easily have been several years younger, possibly by as much as a decade. His face still prompted no actual recognition, although there was something —

Whatever it was, she couldn't place him. She slowed, but kept moving, anxious not to be separated too far from the people up ahead. He paced beside her, slowly gathering his breath before speaking again with obvious discomfort.

'I'm trying to find a David Simmons. I don't know his address, but I was told he lives somewhere around here. Do you —?' As they reached the corner, a fit of coughing took him, bringing him to a halt.

She paused, feeling secure now in the presence of passing traffic and approaching pedestrians, waiting until his coughing subsided.

'I'm sorry, I don't know anyone of that name.'

His response took her completely by surprise. She'd anticipated disappointment, even if only feigned, but instead it was as though she'd delivered a shot of some instant-acting miracle potion that simultaneously stimulated and pacified. His eyes were suddenly alive and steady on her face, their previous nervous flickering stilled. He continued to stare at her intently, but smiling now, a clear expression of intense relief, and something else that could have been —

Surely not — genuine tenderness? She'd been half-prepared for some indication of infatuation, but what she saw implied a depth of feeling that startled and disorientated her. Strangely, though, despite her embarrassment she still felt no alarm; her own initial mild disquiet suddenly replaced by a sensation that she didn't immediately identify, but that somehow echoed what she saw on his face.

She began to inch away from him.

'I'm sorry, I can't help you.' She forced a smile and moved on, reaching the nearby bus stop as a bus drifted to a halt there and people began to climb aboard. She followed them, glancing back to where he stood, his face still illuminated by the transforming smile.

She found a vacant seat and sat down, staring out of the window, oblivious of the passing scenery. What on Earth had all that been about? she wondered. Apart from the mystery of his obvious interest in her, she was totally bemused by the abrupt change that had come over both of them at the time of her denial of knowledge; her seeming inability to help him had contradictorily transformed his anxiety into relief and simultaneously allayed her own, replacing it with the sensation that she now acknowledged.

Although she was childless, and had yet to form a strong romantic attachment, she was fully aware that normal maternal instincts were a strong part of her nature. Back there, though, she'd briefly experienced them to a startling degree, an acute feeling of protectiveness towards a complete stranger who at the very least was twenty years her senior, a surge of empathy that had made no sense at the time and now felt like nothing more than an embarrassing absurdity.

Get a grip, girl, she told herself. Save it for when the time comes, if it ever does. She was still trying to make sense of it all when she finished her journey and crossed the road towards the staff entrance of the hospital.

★ ★ ★

The minute-hand of the clock above the magazine rack had almost reached the number eleven as he pulled the phone towards him and rested his hand on top of it, following what by now had become a sardonic daily ritual.

Seconds later, it rang. He picked it up and reported on the day's takings, and by the time he'd listened disinterestedly to the owner's customary litany of complaints about the state of his various other business interests and replaced it in its cradle, it was a minute to eight.

That'll be the day, he thought sourly, when he doesn't make sure he's getting his money's worth. And why does he have to tell *me* about his problems? He'd already emptied the till and bagged its contents, and was emerging from behind the counter preparatory to taking them down to the basement safe when he glanced outside and saw the car slide into the pool of light illuminating the forecourt.

He swore, disgustedly. Given another ten seconds or so and he'd have locked the door and reversed the card to 'CLOSED', but doing that now could provoke an argument with somebody who might be prepared to engage in a lengthy exchange that would only delay him further.

He reluctantly moved back behind the

counter, depositing the takings bag beneath it, and watching as the driver climbed slowly out of the car, walked around it to the nearest pump, unhooked the hose, and stuck the nozzle into the jerry can he'd been carrying. A couple of bucks' worth. Well, at least it should be a quick sale. He switched on the pump and waited, drumming his fingers impatiently on the counter top.

A minute or so later, the man entered, carrying the can, bringing with it the reek of gasoline. Jesus, he thought, irritably. If he had to bring it with him, at least he could have put the cap back on first. He switched off the pump, and turned. 'That'll be a dollar eighty-five.'

The man made no move to produce any money. He placed the can on the floor, then slowly straightened, his right hand wedged in the pocket of his raincoat, staring at him with feverish eyes set deep in a leaden face. He coughed several times, a lightly hoarse sound.

Jesus, he thought, this is one sick-looking guy; more like a walking corpse than a living being. And why was he staring at him like that? He felt a twinge of unease. He said again, 'That'll be a dollar eighty-five.'

The man cleared his throat. 'You're David Simmons.'

It was a statement, delivered flatly, with no hint of query. So that was it, he thought. He knew him from someplace, although there was no recognition as far as he was concerned. Maybe he was the father of someone he knew, some background figure that had registered him without it being reciprocal on his own part.

He manufactured a smile. 'That's right. I guess we must've met sometime.'

The man nodded, slowly. Equally slowly, he pulled his right hand from his raincoat pocket.

The gun he was holding glinted threateningly in the fluorescent glare of the room. Speaking in the same tired rasp as before, he said, 'Keep your hands where I can see them, and come out here and lock the door. When you've done that, go to the office and turn on the light, then come back and switch off everything out here: this room, the forecourt lights. If you try to run for it or make any kind of move towards me, I'll shoot. Do you understand?'

In the space of a second his simulated affability had stiffened into frozen alarm. Oh God, he thought, sickly. It was what he'd always feared, stuck out here in the middle of nowhere. If the owner wasn't so remorselessly punctual with his daily check-ups he'd have been out of there at least five minutes before, encouraged to leave early by the absence of traffic; on his way back to town and his date for that evening, safe from —

His mind wavered, a shocking realisation penetrating the panicky fog that filled it. The guy knew his name, recognised him from somewhere! The fact that he hadn't been able to identify him in return might be seen as a purely temporary lapse of memory on his part that might correct itself at any time, automatically making him a particularly dangerous witness to the crime.

'Now, wait a minute.' He raised his hands, swallowing hard. 'I don't know how you know my name, mister, but I swear I never saw you before.'

He stared the man in the eye, willing him to believe him, at the same time fractionally increasing the pressure on his abdomen where it already rested against the counter, praying that this minute movement would be seen as nothing more than emphasising the urgency of his claim. Braced against it, he fished carefully with his right foot. There! He felt the shallow rubber mound of the alarm-button, and pressed down on it with the toe of his shoe. 'Honest to God, I don't know who you are. You must — '

'Don't talk,' the man said. He was suddenly energised, naked hatred clear in his voice, startling in its impact. He raised the gun a little, the knuckle of his trigger-finger gleaming whitely. 'Be quiet, and do what I told you. If you don't, I'll shoot you right now.'

He means it, he thought dazedly. Mother of mercy, he really means it. He inched his way from behind the counter on legs that barely supported him, and began to carry out the man's instructions, desperately trying to ensure that none of his movements provided an excuse for this threat to be carried out.

Had that really been hatred that he'd heard? What could he possibly have done to have invoked such abhorrence? Was he the father of some girl who'd achieved an unwanted pregnancy and named him as the person responsible? Unless he'd used a faulty condom during one of his sexual adventures, he was certain of his lack of guilt as far as such a possibility was concerned. But whatever transgression, imagined or otherwise, might have been responsible for this encounter, there was no doubting that this was no straightforward hold-up. Everything that was happening clearly indicated that a personal element was dictating the situation, that the man with the gun was an inexplicably dangerous adversary whose resentment meant that he was fully prepared to end his life at any time.

He tried to focus his thinking, seek out some solution to this appalling predicament. Had the alarm-bell worked, the signal got through? Even if it had, they were eight miles from Laxton, the nearest town; and the gas station was isolated, nowhere near any other source of law enforcement that he knew of.

His only real hope of early help from the police was if a patrol car wasn't too far away and the message had been relayed. He couldn't count on anything like that, though. Perhaps his only real chance of survival would be to jump the guy if the opportunity presented itself. His throat, already restricted with fear, almost closed at the prospect. The office was cramped, though, so they'd be bound to be close to one another once they were inside. Besides, he was young and strong, and the man was plainly unwell and most likely weakened by his condition. If he could just get a grip on his gun-arm —

As he carefully entered the office, a sudden blow took him on the back of the neck. Retching and half-conscious, he dropped to his knees. Then the second blow came, this time pitching him into smothering darkness.

★ ★ ★

He came to gradually, his head thudding, dully aware of the pain that filled it and of the rancid moistness of his lap and thighs. He was seated on a chair, his legs free, but his arms looped behind it and fastened to its frame. He tugged, weakly, and felt the edge of the tape that bound them dig into his wrists.

The man was facing him, seated on the swivel-chair that was normally behind the desk. There was no sign of the gun now, but the open can of petrol rested by his right foot, somehow a significant threat that terrifyingly penetrated his still-sluggish consciousness.

He tugged feebly at the tape again, feeling sick and dreadfully afraid.

He said, quaveringly, 'Why are you doing this? Have I done something that's offended you real bad? If I have, I swear to God I don't know what it was. Why don't you — ' He stopped, confused by the man's response, the slow side-to-side shaking of his head.

'Not yet.'

Not yet? What could *that* possibly mean?

'If you live,' the man said, 'you'll go on to do great harm. To me, but particularly to someone else. I have to try to prevent that from happening.'

It took several seconds for what had been said to fully penetrate his consciousness; but when it did, his insides, already taut with panic, contracted to a nausea-inducing ball.

He was at the mercy of a lunatic, someone who believed that he could forecast the future, one in which he would commit some unspecified act of cruelty that could only be avoided if he were to die before it could take place! He almost fainted in this state of near-fugue, witnessing a macabre image of himself crouched motionless on a sheet of glass that was barely thick enough to support him, the only thing saving him from falling irrecoverably into the blackly bottomless abyss that yawned beneath it. A single movement, one ill-judged redistribution of his weight, would shatter the glass and pitch him headlong into this passage to inescapable death; he knew it with chilling certainty.

Shuddering uncontrollably, he resurfaced to equally chilling reality: the fume-filled confines of the office and the grey-faced man slumped in the other chair, his mind surely deformed by his deadly fantasy.

Numb with panic, he tried to think. Stall him, that was all he could do. Pray that the alarm signal had got through and that help was on its way. Would reason have any effect, or would it provoke him to impatient anger, actually precipitate what he intended to do? Perhaps it was the only way to stretch the moments, give himself any chance at all of survival.

He'd have to risk it. He swallowed again, desperately trying to lubricate the arid tunnel that his throat had become. 'How do you know what's going to happen in the future? Nobody does, not really. How do you know I'm going to do what you say I am?'

The man stared at him silently for several seconds before speaking. 'Because it's already happened.'

There it was, confirmation of his insanity! His mind groped frantically, trying to find the right words, any argument at all that might pacify this madman.

'But how can it have? You mean you were actually there when I did this thing?'

The man's mouth turned down, grimly. 'Not to witness it directly. But, yes, I was there.'

He ploughed on, doggedly committed now. 'But you'd have to be able to travel through time to know anything like that! Is that what you're saying, that you're from the future, and that you've come back to try and put right whatever it is you say I've done?'

The man nodded, a single duck of the head. 'Yes, that is what I'm saying.'

He means it, he thought sickly. He really believes it. Perhaps attempting to make contact with any possible remaining shreds of reason would be pointless, but for now it was his only hope. He introduced a wheedling note into his voice.

'Look, why not tell me what it is you say I'm going to do? If I know what it is, I won't do it, honest to God I won't.

Wouldn't that make more sense than killing me?' This spoken acknowledgement of the man's intentions was almost a relief. Cards on the table, he thought light-headedly. Why not? In that sense at least, what have I got to lose?

There was another pause, longer this time. He allowed himself the first faint flicker of hope. At least he'd got him thinking, pointed out an option that seemed to have created at least some uncertainty. How could he reinforce that? If he could only —

The man said, 'Do you suffer from nightmares?'

The question took him completely by surprise, seguing almost at once into a surge of relief that was overwhelming.

Of course! That must be what this was, a nightmare brought about by his constant fear that the isolation of the gas station would one day invite criminal intrusion, with this demented scenario its manifestation! None of it was real: the man with his gun and his mad tale, the can of gasoline and its implied threat . . .

He took a deep breath. His dreams

216

occasionally reached a point where he identified them as such, sometimes even enabling him to force himself awake, free himself from their warped settings and events. Now that he'd recognised this torment for what it really was, he should be able to exert at least a degree of control.

He began to tug at the restricting tape again, gradually dismayed by the continuing resistance he encountered. Even at their most threatening, actual physical discomfort was never part of his dreams. He blinked repeatedly, willing himself to wake, suddenly intensely conscious again of his surroundings and what they contained: the grey-faced man confronting him, staring at him with feverish eyes, the overpowering reek of gasoline that filled the small room.

No dream. He sagged in his chair, his heart accelerating again to its previous thudding gallop, an onslaught that this time felt as though it might tear itself free of its arterial moorings.

Keep talking, he told himself dully. It's all you can do. Talk and pray.

He stonewalled. 'Why do you want to know that? What have nightmares got to do with any of this?'

The man shifted slightly in his chair, a movement that somehow implied more than simply physical discomfort. He said, slowly, 'This is an unprecedented situation. It contains factors that make accurate prediction — difficult.' He fell silent, his face pensive.

Again, hesitation. He snatched at this straw.

'Are you saying you're not sure you've got this right? That there's a chance that killing me won't prevent this thing you say I'm going to do from happening?'

The man moistened his lips. 'A degree of uncertainty's involved. Whether or not it can be resolved — '

'So you're not sure? If you're not, how can you justify doing it?'

The deep-sunk eyes stared at him, broodingly. 'If I don't, the guarantee of what you'll do remains.'

He took a deep breath. 'But you don't know for sure that it'll work, you've just admitted that. That means you could be committing murder totally unnecessarily! Do you really want to take that kind of — '

He faltered to a halt, abruptly gripped by a fresh onrush of terror as he saw the change in the man's expression and demeanour. It was as though a sudden draught of icy air had entered the room, dispersing the fog of doubt that he'd desperately been trying to nurture, and simultaneously leaving the flicker of hope guttering perilously close to extinguishment.

Oh God, what had he done? He shuddered, feeling the cold envelop him like a freezing shroud.

'That'll be the culmination of what you'll do, commit unnecessary murder.' There was no trace of hesitation on the leaden face now. The man's eyes were coldly certain again, and unadulterated hatred was clear in his voice. 'You're destined to kill someone who's done everything in their power to help you. If the uncertainty can be resolved, it won't only mean that that person will survive, you'll no longer be guilty of committing this outrage. I realise, of course, that this is no consolation to you now, but it'll also mean that you'll be spared a bitter, self-inflicted end.' A twisted grimace flickered briefly across his face. 'By killing you now, I may even be saving your soul.'

His soul? The existence of such an abstract thing was something that he'd never seriously considered, and even if it did exist it was of little concern to him at that moment. His life and the sensual pleasures that it offered were what he wanted, not to be meaninglessly despatched into some unknown limbo, where it might well transpire that redemption was a myth and the harsh reality was that all things ended.

How long had it been since the commencement of this purgatory? There was a clock on the wall behind him, but positioned as he was there was no chance of his seeing it. Ten minutes, fifteen, more? He had no idea how long he'd been unconscious, so it could have been considerably longer; surely long enough for help to have arrived by now.

At the time of his fumbling use of the

alarm-button it had felt as though he'd managed to depress it fully, but what if it had developed a fault? He felt a fresh wave of despair. Maybe help wasn't coming at all, and his fate had been sealed by a bad wiring connection or such. He stifled a sob. You have to keep him talking for as long as possible, he told himself; try to reason some sanity into his disordered brain. It's probably your only chance now.

Through parched lips, he said, 'I don't understand any of this. You say I'm going to murder someone, but you haven't told me who or why. Who are you, anyway, and what makes you so sure it's me who's going to do it? You didn't actually see it happen, you've admitted that, so how can you be certain that it'll be me and not somebody else?'

There was no instant reply. The man coughed frequently now, his already-laboured breathing clearly aggravated by the fumes emanating from the open can by his feet. At last, he said, 'You'd derive no comfort from knowing any of those things.'

He persisted. 'It's only fair that I know. Right now I haven't harmed this person, and that means I'm innocent! I've committed no crime, and I wouldn't harm anybody, I just wouldn't!' He repeated his earlier plea. 'Tell me who it is I'm supposed to kill, and I won't do it, I swear on my mother's grave I won't!'

A grotesque smile formed on the grey face. The man emitted a cough-punctuated travesty of a laugh that continued for a while before he spoke again.

'A singularly empty promise, since your mother's alive and well and will outlive you by many years.' His contempt was manifest. 'In any event, that kind of assurance is meaningless, because if you live circumstances will eventually guarantee that you commit this atrocity. Simply the fact that killing you now may prevent it means that I have no other acceptable choice.' He studied him thoughtfully, then shrugged. 'I suppose it's only reasonable that you should be told. Death can often be seen as pointless, and at least it'll make you understand why yours will have meaning. Mine, too; a matter of secondary importance, but I find it consoling.'

He lowered his gaze, staring blankly at the floor as he talked, his narrative punctuated with regular pauses to enable him to gather his breath. 'My parents had a troubled marriage. My father was frequently unfaithful, but most damage was done by his seemingly uncontrollable rages. He was unemployed for much of the time, and his frustration often led to his using violence towards my mother and me. He would often beat me for no good reason, and he struck her many times, usually for defending me. She once told me that this aspect of his behaviour was brought on by his dreams, nightmares that he couldn't articulate clearly because they contained terrors that he couldn't identify, and that we had to sympathise and not condemn him.'

At least he'd achieved his initial aim, to keep him talking. He said, carefully, 'It sounds like he was sick. Did your mother ever try to persuade him to get help? Psychiatry, that kind of thing?'

'He refused to consider treatment. I imagine it was because he was terrified of having to face the things that were concealed in his dreams. Perhaps he was afraid that exposure to them would be the road to insanity, and as long as they remained hidden he was safe from that.'

'Why didn't your mother leave him, get the two of you away someplace where he wasn't likely to find you?'

Again the grey features twisted into a smile, this time a bitter one.

'Compassion was a strong part of her nature, and it was also clear that at the very least she'd deluded herself into believing that she still loved him, despite his infidelity and violent outbursts. He possessed the usual qualities that encourage us to make fools of ourselves in that respect; good looks and charm, which in his case was an earthy and purely superficial attribute that he turned on and off like a tap whenever it suited him. It was a relationship that I never understood, and never could; but love's frequently an irrational emotion, of course, incomprehensible to the onlooker.' The man shrugged, wearily. 'Perhaps I'm underestimating the depth of her feelings for him; but whatever they were, she still recognised that he posed a risk as far as I was concerned, and lived in constant fear for my safety. Despite that, she felt it was her duty to stay with him, in the hope that eventually she'd be able to persuade him to accept the need for the kind of outside help that could exorcise his demons. After I was born she gave up her job to be with me until I reached school age. When I was old enough to be safely out of his way during the day, she did part-time work whenever it was available.'

He did his best to introduce a sympathetic note into his voice. 'That must've been tough, raising you with money only coming in sometimes.'

'She'd inherited some from an uncle who'd died shortly before she met my father. Whenever it became necessary, she dipped into that. Just before I reached my teens, it had all gone. When it had, he looked for more elsewhere, which came as no surprise to me.' Cynicism coloured the rasping voice. 'At a very young age I'd realised that he saw her principally as an

225

accommodating meal-ticket who was illogically prepared to put up with his womanising and ill-treatment.

'At the time he had a temporary delivery job that took him to other towns in the county. When he was in Gallerton he met a woman customer who ran her own successful small business, and had also received a substantial settlement at the time of her divorce. He had, as you'll have already gathered, a way with women, and he courted her, convincing her that he was unattached. Although her money was the initial attraction, after a while he found himself in a more serious relationship than he'd anticipated.

'He decided to leave us, but on the day that he was packing his belongings my mother returned home earlier than expected. He was furious at being caught in this way, and there was an argument that escalated to the point where in order to hurt and humiliate her even further he told her why he was going. My mother was stung into responding by telling him that she'd find this woman, then tell her the facts of his marital status and of the way he treated us. Faced with the possibility of losing both his new amour, and the improvement to his personal circumstances her money would bring, he panicked.'

The cynicism had gone now. Raw emotion had replaced it, thickening his voice into a relentlessly harsh sound, unsteady with deep feeling.

'He beat my mother unconscious and set fire to the apartment, seeing this as a means of both ridding himself of her and destroying the evidence of his brutality, hoping to convince the authorities that she died accidentally after somehow causing it herself. But the rescue team managed to recover her body before it could be burned. The coroner's report concluded that she'd been alive when he started the fire, and that her death had been caused by smoke inhalation.'

He talked on, temporarily lost in his memories; about his father's arrest and subsequent confession when confronted with the testimony of a neighbour who'd detected smoke before seeing him leave the apartment; the court's condemnation of his utter callousness towards her and his total lack of regard for the building's other occupants; his imprisonment for first-degree murder; and his suicide several months after his incarceration.

He slowly shrank in his chair as the man's story unfolded. Dear Christ, he thought, appalled. Surely he can't be thinking that I'm — ? No, that can't be right! He hastily slammed a shutter closed in his mind, and plunged in again.

'I don't understand how anybody could do something like that. I guess he got what was coming to him, all right. So what happened to you afterwards?'

'I was taken by my mother's parents. Shortly before her marriage to my father, something that they'd strongly advised against, they moved several hundred miles away, and after that underlined their disapproval by rarely contacting her. Her misguided loyalty to my father meant that they'd never known the truth about his treatment of her and me. After her death, they attempted to assuage their consciences for ignoring her by treating me as the son they never had.

'They were fundamentally decent people, and deeply regretted what they saw as their sin of omission. From that point on my life was stable, and I buried myself in my school studies, principally as a means of trying to blot out the horrors that I'd gone through before. I had a natural bent for the sciences, and eventually became a researcher in the quantum physics field, finally working on a program that's made it possible for us to step back in time. That's how I'm here, of course; against all the rules governing use of the process, I should add.'

Clearly animated by this ostensible reference to his work, the grey-faced man continued talking, about the existing limitations of what had been achieved so far and how they hoped it would develop in the future, temporarily engrossed in his fanciful exposition.

His relief at this unexpected diversion was short-lived. Insistently now, the thought that had intruded so jarringly moments before returned, brusquely sweeping aside his initial rejection, demanding acceptance. He tried desperately to dismiss it again, but this time it refused to retreat, its glaring obviousness peremptorily swamping his resistance and rapidly forming an impenetrable barrier against any possibility of denial

It's true, he thought, dazedly. Dear Christ, the crazy bastard thinks he's talking about *me*! For some insane reason he's selected me as the target for his delusion, identified me as the monster he's been describing!

My name! Of course, that's it! He's confused me with somebody else called David Simmons! He sobbed at the deadly irony of this coincidence. It left unexplained how the man's tortured memories had deformed themselves into his belief that he'd travelled back in time to wreak vengeance on his parent, but perhaps his sickness was responsible.

Whatever the nature or cause of his obvious illness, his condition could have affected his mind as well as his body, drawn him into this feverish fantasy. Maybe he really was involved in some scientific programme that was investigating the possibility of time-travel; and if he was, it was perfectly logical to assume that his afflicted state had resulted in his conviction that they'd succeeded, and that his dream of revenge would become a reality.

Yes, that made its own twisted kind of sense. But even though he'd reasoned out the most probable explanation for this lunatic belief, he still had to face up to the obdurate fact that words were still his only weapon, an acceptance of the meagreness of his memory that left him feeling hollow, teetering on the very edge of despair.

He dragged himself away from it with every ounce of mental effort that he could muster. Use them, then, he urged himself, exhaustedly. Use them, and keep on using them as long as possible. Maybe help's still coming after all, but either way you have to keep him talking. Whatever you do, though, don't push, or try to force the issue. Challenging him was a waste of breath, so simply denying that you're his future father won't get you any place. What you've got to do is coax him, gently lead him to the realisation that there's no way you could possibly be the murderous bully he thinks you are; convince him that you genuinely are appalled by what he's told you, and that the whole thing's a terrible mistake.

Barely conscious of what was being said during the man's discourse, he suddenly realised that it had ended. Caught off-guard, he swallowed hastily, and blurted: 'You've had a real tough time, mister, that's for sure.' *What to say, what to say? Quick, quick, you mustn't hesitate!* He seized on the first thought that came to him.

'Do you know what he was going to do about you if he'd gotten away with it? You say he'd fooled this woman into believing that he didn't have any kind of ties, so he couldn't have taken you along with him. I guess that'd have been the last thing he'd have wanted to do, anyway.'

Was that anger he saw again beginning to cloud the leaden face? Oh God, he thought, sickly, am I doing this all wrong?

Panic froze his imagination. Helplessly locked on the course that his inattention had hurried him into taking, he babbled on. 'I mean, was he just going to disappear after a while, simply dump you, or was he planning to kill you too before he took off? Either way that'd have brought the police — ' He faltered to a halt, shocked into horrified silence by the now-unmistakable effect of his words.

The grey features were dark with fury, a reaction that brushed aside his clumsy edifice of interest like so much matchwood. He quailed before the basilisk glare, despairingly recognising that instead of easing the man towards acknowledgement of his error, his attempt at ingratiation had in all probability just confirmed his own certain death.

The man said, 'Trying to change my mind by undermining my determination with a show of interest and mock sympathy is quite pointless, believe me.' His voice was harshly implacable, with a vicious edge to it that cut into his consciousness like a razor-edged knife. 'Even so, I'm going to answer your questions, so that before you die you appreciate the lengths that he was prepared to go to, to achieve what he thought of as his freedom.'

His hands, which had been moving restlessly on the arms of his chair, now gripped them tightly. 'Before taking his own life he wrote me a note; but in view of my age and its contents, it was withheld from me. It was only when I reached my late teens and asked my grandparents if he'd mentioned me before doing away with himself that they reluctantly told me of its existence. They'd kept it, and since by then I'd matured beyond my years, they decided that I was capable of facing the truth, and gave it to me.'

The rasping voice was gradually thickening again.

'I'd naively assumed that it would contain at least some hint of remorse, perhaps even a request for forgiveness for the things he'd done. Instead, I found myself reading the self-pitying ranting of someone who clearly only considered his own wants and appetites. In it, he admitted that in the panic of the moment he'd overlooked the problem that I'd pose afterwards; and told me that if he hadn't allowed himself to be rushed into doing what he did, he'd have waited until I returned home from school, and then subjected me to the same treatment that he'd meted out to my mother before starting the fire. With both of us dead, he could have gone to this woman unencumbered: able, in his own words, to make a clean, fresh start. Even if he hadn't been unlucky enough to be caught, he said, he couldn't have killed or deserted me so soon after my mother's death without arousing suspicion.

'This meant that my continuing existence would have robbed him of what he wanted, and he damned me for it, saying that he wished I'd never been born.'

Rage and contempt clotted the grating voice.

'These twisted regrets for what might have been were the last outpourings of a sick and sadistic mind, before he ended his own wretched life with a knotted shirt-sleeve around his neck; a suitably shabby finish to a life that should have ended many years earlier, before he could inflict his brutality on someone who wasted her own life by convincing herself that he deserved her love and tolerance and pity.'

Provoked by the vehemence of these final words, a paroxysm of coughing wracked the man for a full minute. When it eventually subsided, he sat slumped in his chair, breathing deep, shuddering breaths, his eyes closed and his grey features now drawn to the point of emaciation.

He wrenched desperately at his bonds, shaking his head wildly in repeated denial. 'No, no, you've got this all wrong!' He was gabbling, almost incoherent, all thought of gradual persuasion abandoned. 'I'm not him, I'm *not*! There are Simmonses all over, don't you see? It's a common name, like Smith and Jones and Brown and Green! In any case, I couldn't do any of those things! I couldn't hurt people like that, especially if they were my own family!' He writhed helplessly, sweat and tears intermingling as they streamed down his face. 'I couldn't do things like that, I just *know* I couldn't!'

The man slowly roused himself again. Apart from the visible tremor of his hands, now resting claw-like on the arms of his chair, he was suddenly calm, exhibiting no sign of the passion that had possessed him a short while before.

'The seeds of extreme cruelty are in all of us. Circumstances dictate whether or not they ever influence our behaviour.' The sunken eyes watched his contortions detachedly. 'History's shown us that, subjected to the right stimulus, they can turn perfectly rational and humane beings into savages, capable of atrocities that would normally be beyond their imagining. The desire for retribution can become that kind of cancer, something that I can personally vouch for. As to your identity, do you think I'd forget my father's face, his voice? Believe me, they're like festering sores in my memory.' He shrugged. 'You may well be telling the truth about yourself as you are now, but unless you die before these things can happen, that's the unspeakable creature that you'll become, for whatever reason. Remember, I've seen and suffered the abominable things that you'll do, and I'm going to change them if I can. The only chance of that is by killing you, which is why I must do it.'

The words struck him like a barrage of heavy stones, remorseless and unforgiving, stunning him once more to near-insensibility. He sagged beneath their onslaught, again conjuring up the earlier image of himself crouched in petrified stillness on the flimsy transparency suspended over bottomless darkness; only now this wafer of protection was inexorably tilting as though on some unseen axis. He felt himself slipping and opened his mouth to scream when something halted his slide, a mental handhold that he clung to with one final surge of hope.

'That can't be true, it *can't*!' He was shouting now, his voice hoarse and ragged with desperation. 'But even if it was, don't you see what killing me would mean? *You* won't exist, because you couldn't. If I die now, there's no way that this woman and I could become your parents, don't you *see* that?'

Through the water filming his eyes, he again saw the travesty of a smile distort the leaden face.

The man said, 'The classic paradox. If I kill my father, what happens to me?' He laughed, a wheezing ululation that almost instantly degenerated into another fit of coughing during which he leaned forward, his elbows on his knees and his head lowered, until it petered into near-silence. When he looked up again his face was streaked with perspiration, and the fever in his eyes was brighter than before.

'I'm sick, as you can see. If this experiment succeeds, the improbable event of my surviving its outcome can only be for a short while; but whatever happens, the continuation of my life is a matter of no real concern. I have no dependants, which in these circumstances is a blessing; and in any case, the fact that it was necessary for me to bypass what would normally be essential parts of the transfer procedures that have enabled me to be here now means that there's no possibility of returning to my own time. This leaves me with few options, but the truth is that my own death will be a merciful release from an existence that for some time now I've found barely tolerable, and which eventually convinced me that before it was too late I had to try and right the dreadful wrong that you'll do if left alive. If I should somehow survive, shortly afterwards I'll follow you, although a bullet will spare me the agony that in the future you'd be prepared to inflict on my mother and myself, and which you're about to experience.' He broke off again, breathing heavily, his tongue flicking repeatedly across his lips and his eyes once more closed.

The by-now deafening thunder of his heart had smothered much of this spelling-out of intent, but enough of it had still penetrated his understanding for him to have recognised the note of finality it contained. His bowels, long in turmoil, surrendered their contents, the stench of this shame invading his nostrils as he rocked and swayed, pleading, his voice a shrill whimper. 'No, no, you can't — dear Christ, I'm begging you — ' He broke down, choking on the words. His head sank onto his chest, and he wept uncontrollably for the existence that he was about to lose.

The man's eyes opened again, and

when he spoke it was slowly and quietly.

'Whether or not you believe what I've told you about our relationship, you've clearly decided that I'm insane. Perhaps I am a little, although not in the way that I imagine you're thinking. I've lived with this hatred and desire for revenge for so long now that it may well have poisoned my mind to that extent, but it doesn't alter the truth of what you've just learned. I did, of course, give you fair warning that knowing the facts wouldn't comfort you in any way, but your insistence persuaded me that you had a right to be told them.' He took a deep, rasping breath, and raised a hand in what was clearly a gesture signalling completion.

'Now that you have, and despite the uncertainty involved, I see no point in waiting any longer to attempt to fulfil what I consider to be my justifiable obligation.'

He reached into his coat pocket. When his hand re-emerged, it was holding a small white tube with a rounded metal end. He depressed a button in its side, and the domed tip began to glow redly.

Closing his eyes again, he said, 'May God have mercy on both our souls.' He leaned down and grasped the handle of the can with his free hand, tilting it and directing its contents across the floor.

Apart from his failed attempts to tear himself free of the tape binding his wrists, until that moment he had more or less accepted the futility of attempting any kind of physical response. Now, confronted with these things — the white tube and its glowing end, the tilted can and the steady release of what it contained — something snapped inside his head, abruptly wrenching him out of this paralysis.

He shrieked a wordless emanation of terror, sheer animal instinct dictating his movements as the gasoline flooded beneath and around him. Spreading his feet beyond the width of the chair and dragging them parallel with its front legs, he threw all his weight forward, somehow achieving enough momentum to enable him to lurch upwards into a crouching stance. As he did so, startlingly, muffled sounds from beyond the closed door impinged faintly on his wavering consciousness; the crash of shattering glass, shouts, the hurried thud of approaching footsteps, intrusions that provoked the grey-faced man into rising unsteadily to his feet, his head turned towards them and his jaw agape.

Doubled over, the chair angled above him like the skeleton of some bizarre carapace, he shuffled frantically towards the door, colliding with the grey-faced man and knocking the can from his hand as he passed him. Just before reaching the door, his feet slithered from under him. As he twisted and fell, he caught a fleeting glimpse of it miraculously swinging open to reveal the uniformed figure of a patrolman staring into the room.

Hands grasped him and dragged him through the opening, away from the creeping carpet of searing flame that licked at his feet and legs. Before retreating into blessed unconsciousness, his last sight was of the inferno of light and heat that now filled the office; and the last sounds he heard, the agonised screams that rose from its depths.

*   *   *

The two doctors were standing just inside the doors when she entered the ward. As he passed them she overheard a fragment of their conversation, meaningless at the time, but which she recalled later.

' — difficult to say. He may come out of it eventually, of course, but if he does, I think we can anticipate a very long haul. One way and another, the best thing — '

It was the first time that she'd been seconded to the burns unit, currently understaffed due to a virus that had laid low two of its regular staff; and the sister-in-charge talked her through procedures and practices before taking her with her on her own normal morning round.

The curtains had been pulled around the fourth bed they visited. The sister peered inside, then closed them again.

'He's asleep. There'd be no point in disturbing him now. He's been through a lot, poor boy. Somebody tied him up at the gas station where he worked and then started a fire, the police don't know why. They found a body afterwards, or what was left of one. It might even have been the person responsible, I suppose. Hoist with his own petard if it was.' She grimaced. 'Anyway, this lad's got second-degree burns to his lower legs, but his big problem's post-traumatic stress disorder. He remembers everything up to the afternoon of the day it happened, but nothing at all about the actual incident. Mr. Crossley says it's possible that he'll never remember any of it, which would be a blessing in some ways, I suppose.'

They moved on to the next bed.

'How are you this morning, John? You're looking chirpy enough. This is Nurse Parker.' She exchanged smiles with the man in the bed. 'She'll be changing your dressings later. She's got the gentle touch, I'm told, so there shouldn't be any need to fuss like you usually do.'

It wasn't until late morning that she saw him for the first time. The curtains were still drawn when she finished re-bandaging the man in the next bed, and then checked to see if he wanted anything.

He was still asleep, his head turned sideways on the pillow. Her pulse quickened a little, a reaction that brought a slight flush to her cheeks. Don't be ridiculous, she scolded herself. Even so, he undeniably possessed the kind of looks that had always appealed to her: darkly attractive, with long-lashed eyes and gently wavy hair, rumpled now. It certainly would have been a crime in more ways than one to have killed him, she thought protectively. What possible reason could there have been for such a brutal act? She recalled the sister's account of his terrifying ordeal that had earlier aroused her own deep sympathy, despite his concealed anonymity at the time, and which had now become magnified at the sight of him.

She closed the curtains again and went to the foot of the bed, unhooking the chart here, the name she saw on it instantly flicking at her memory.

David Simmons? Hadn't that been the name of the person the sick-looking stranger who'd accosted her a few days before had claimed to be looking for? What a weird coincidence, she thought. The encounter itself had been odd enough, especially the startling reversal that had resulted from her denial of knowledge, almost as though her inability to help him had relieved him of some distressing burden.

Well, now she did know a David Simmons, or would do very shortly. Smiling at the thought, she replaced the chart and was beginning to move on when she heard moaning from behind the closed curtains. She pulled them open again, finding him stirring agitatedly in his sleep, sweat beginning to bead his brow.

As abruptly as it had started, the sound stopped and the movement stilled. A nightmare, she thought. Perhaps the doctors were wrong after all, and he was beginning to remember his ordeal. Poor boy. He clearly needed special care, the ministrations of someone who was truly concerned for his welfare, in what was bound to be a difficult future for him.

She wondered if he already had some-one like that: a mother, perhaps a wife?

She gently removed the sweat with a tissue as she studied his handsome face, again resting peacefully on the pillow.

THE END